GREED

THE DARK KINGS

Greed by Nikki Rome

Published by Rome Publishing Group

www.NikkiRome.com

© 2022 Nikki Rome

This book is a work of fiction. Names, characters, places, and incidents are products of

the author's imagination or are used fictionally. Any resemblance to actual people,

living or dead, events or locations is entirely coincidental.

For permissions contact:

Info@NikkiRome.com

Cover by Alt19 Creative

CONTENT WARNINGS

Content Warnings: The Dark Kings is a high steam, high action dark romance series. The following content warnings should be considered before reading them: Dealing with previous trauma, assault, miscarriage, murder, sex trafficking, drug use, depression, anxiety, PTSD, bipolar disorder, gun violence, kidnapping, sexism, prostitution, elements of BDSM such as impact play and restraints, electro stimulation, knife play, primal play, CGL relationship, Shabari, profanity and sexually explicit scenes. This is a Why Choose romance. If you have any questions please reach out to the author directly at info @nikkirome.com.

CHAPTER ONE
MAYA

I don't know why I bother planning shit, because everything always goes to hell. My most recent set of plans only lasted about three years. Those plans got me out of the house I'm currently standing in and out on my own. Those plans also helped me gain confidence in myself for the first time in my life. Now, because of one asshole, I'm standing in the last place I want to be. Anton Tirelli was a memory I was happy to leave behind, but now he was the only person I knew could help me.

"He'll be with you soon. Are you sure there isn't anything I can get you?"

"No, Marybeth, I'm fine, thank you." Anton's live-in housekeeper had been one of my favorite people back in the day. Now she looked at me with pity in her eyes and a sad smile on her face. I watched as the elderly woman made her way back towards the kitchen while I stood in the foyer waiting for Anton. I didn't want to go any further into the house. It would bring up too many memories that I just couldn't deal with after the night I'd had. It was a total shit show and my face was still throbbing from where Eddie hit me. I wasn't surprised Marybeth looked at me the way she did. It's not like I stopped to look in a mirror, but I could feel the blood crusted on my skin and could see the dirt under my nails. My hair was likely ruined from nearly being pulled from my scalp, but the only thing I was concerned about at the time was making it out alive.

"Maya?" His voice was deep and sent a chill up my spine. The same voice that used to whisper to me late at night and tell me he'd protect me at all costs was the same voice that told me to leave him and never look back. I turned to see Anton standing in the hallway and with one look at me, he rushed forward, reaching out and holding my face in his oversized hands, inspecting the damage.

"Who did this to you?"

"It doesn't matter." I said, trying to push him away. His physical touch was too much to bear. He stepped back and lowered his arms and his hands fisted at his sides.

"Then why are you here?"

"I need your help."

"Clearly."

"I don't... fuck... never mind, I should never have come here." I turned to the door only to feel his hand grasp my wrist, pulling me back.

"Maya, wait. I'm sorry."

I turned back and could see his internal struggle. His facial features had softened as he looked down at me, but anger still radiated off of him. I hoped the anger was for the person who did this to me and not for me. With the way we left things, it was hard to tell. I wasn't lying when I said I shouldn't have shown up here, but it wasn't like I had any other options.

"What do you need?" he asked, sensing my hesitance in walking away again.

"I fucked up and now I need help to get out of it."

"Come sit down. I'll have Marybeth bring in something to drink. Do you want to get cleaned up?"

"No, I don't know how much time I have. It's better if I don't stay in one place for very long."

Anton only ever heard what he wanted to hear and the fact that I said no wasn't something that registered. He pulled me gently by the arm and directed me to sit on the large soft leather sectional that we spent countless hours on over the years.

"Sit and tell me what happened."

I watched as he took his phone out of his pocket and sent off a quick text, then he stood over me like some sort of monster waiting to jump on its prey. His intimidation tactics worked on a lot of people, but it never worked on me and he knew it. I had no idea what he was trying to accomplish, but it was a waste of time. I wasn't afraid of Anton. It was the other devils in the city that gave me nightmares.

"You can sit, you know."

"I'm fine. What are you running from?"

"Tommy Marconi."

"The pimp?"

"People don't use the term pimp anymore."

"If it looks like shit and it smells like shit, then it's shit. Why would you be running from Tommy?"

"I killed one of his johns."

"You what?"

"It wasn't on purpose. The guy was violent and out of control. I couldn't get away from him and I grabbed the only thing I could reach."

"Which was what?"

"His knife."

"I see. Maybe you should start from the beginning because I'm lost. Why in the world would you be in a situation where you couldn't get away from one of Tommy's johns?"

"I've been working for him since the club closed."

Anton's face turned red, and he looked as if he was going to explode. The only thing that kept that from happening was Marybeth walking into the living room carrying a tray of drinks, snacks and a first aid kit.

"Here you go, sweetheart," she said, placing the tray in front of me and sitting down to open the first aid box. She pulled a damp cloth from her pocket and carefully turned my face to hers while she wiped away some of the crusted blood. It hurt like hell, but I tried my best not to wince.

After a minute or so of Anton pacing and Marybeth fussing over my cuts and bruises, she turned to him. "We should call the doctor."

"NO! No, I'm fine. Really."

"Let me see," he said as he came closer to us. He leaned forward, and I felt his warm, minty breath against my skin. The smell of his cologne brought back a slew of memories I wasn't prepared for. Some were good, others bad, but none of them wanted. I pushed myself to my feet, causing him to back up.

"I'm fine. Please. I just... need you to help me get out of the city. Out of the country would be better."

"You're not going anywhere. If you want my help, then you do what I say. I want the whole story, Maya, not the bullshit abridged version. Are you telling me you've been turning tricks for Tommy for that last three years?"

"The pay is good."

"The pay? If you needed money, why didn't you just come home?" he yelled loud enough to make Marybeth jump in her seat.

"Home? To you? Don't you remember throwing me out of here? Or was that someone else?"

"I didn't throw you out of here! You left."

"I don't have time for this. Can you help me or not?"

Anton looked at me as if he wanted to strangle me and, in that moment, I shared the sentiment. I glared at him as he shook his head and looked to Marybeth, ignoring me completely.

"Marybeth, can you take Maya to her room so she can take a shower and change?"

"Of course. Come on, sweetheart, let's get you cleaned up."

There was no getting through to him when he was like this. Against my better judgement, I followed her down the long hallways that housed mine and Anton's joint bedrooms. I always wanted my own space, but he didn't want me far from him. After about a million arguments over it, he hired a contractor to build a door between the two bedrooms. A door that I felt was a waste of money, but one that put his mind to ease. He was so proud of himself the day I came home from work and he had finished renovating a room for me with a separate entrance. I smiled at the memory as Marybeth pulled the keys she kept attached to her belt out and unlocked the bedroom I hadn't seen in years.

"He never comes in here anymore. I think it makes him too sad now."

"Why would you say that?"

"He misses you deeply Maya, even though he'd never admit it. I keep it cleaned for you. The clothes you left behind are still hanging in the closet. I guess we both always hoped you'd find your way home."

My eyes stung with tears and I looked away from the kind woman who had become a motherly figure to the both of us so long ago. When Anton's mother died and his father began working for the Corsetti Family, Marybeth became the one constant in both of our lives.

"Thank you Marybeth. I won't take long."

"I'll wait for you in the living room just in case you need anything."

As soon as she stepped from the room, the tears that had been burning in my eyes fell. I'd give anything to get back the life we all had here, but so much had gone wrong it was tarnished with more bad memories than good ones. I crossed the room and put my purse down on my bed before stripping out of my dirty, bloodied clothes. They weren't even worth trying to salvage, so I dropped them into the wastebasket in the bathroom and started the water. While I waited for it to warm up, I opened the drawer that used to hold everything I needed to get ready and found a new toothbrush in its package with a small tube of toothpaste. I scrubbed my teeth clean, took my hair down from the ponytail it was in, and finally risked a look in the mirror.

Marybeth was right. I probably should be in a hospital right now. My eye was nearly swollen shut and the bruise on the side of my face had turned an angry purple color. My eyebrow had split, causing most of the blood. The only thing that hurt more than my headache was the bruising around my ribs. I touched my side gingerly and winced in pain. The kick to my center was something I'd be feeling for a long time. Breathing had been difficult since the adrenaline wore off and now I knew why. Tommy was going to be livid when he realized I'd got away from his goons. His greedy ass would never let me go, no matter how much I begged.

I stepped under the warm water and whimpered in pain. Even the feel of the soft spray hurt. My scalp stung where the water hit it and after I rinsed away the crusted blood from my face, a steady stream continued to get into my eye. Any other day, the familiar scent of her soaps and shampoos could calm me, but tonight it only made me want to cry harder. I washed up and stood there until the tears finally subsided. I was so tired of being tough, so tired of getting my ass kicked. None of it seemed worth it anymore. When I got out and dried off, I found everything in my closet that I had left. The day I packed, I tore the place apart, shoving things into a suitcase and not caring about the mess I left behind. Marybeth must have cleaned everything and rehung my clothes. I grabbed a pair of stretchy pants from the drawer and a hoodie from the shelf. I got dressed and carefully brushed out my hair before heading back out into the house to face Anton's anger.

Seeing him tonight after avoiding him for so long cracked something open in my heart. That small sliver of hope that maybe, just maybe, we could get back to where we were before all the drama kept creeping up and my mind was doing everything it could to protect me from him. When your childhood best friend becomes your lover, shit gets complicated. We knew too much about each other and instead of allowing it to make us stronger, we used it to tear each other apart. When the bad finally outweighed the good, I had no choice but to leave. But things were different now. When his father died the rumors started. People said he changed. He was different. Too much loss could kill a man, but Anton was the strongest man I knew.

CHAPTER TWO

ANTON

Of all the things Maya could have been doing, she'd spent the last three years with Tommy Marconi. Even hearing his name made my skin crawl. Tommy was the absolute scum of the earth. The only good thing about him was he knew to stay far away from me. That was probably why I never got wind of her working for him. Tommy sulked in the shadows and pretended like he ran his little corner of the city. He didn't. The only man running New York right now was Dante Corsetti. The son of the late Mario Corsetti, who my father spent most of this life working for. Until they killed him for it.

When Marybeth told me she was in the foyer, I thought it had to be a joke. The tears in her eyes and hope in her small smile reminded me she'd never joke about something like that. Maya was like a daughter to her and it had devastated Marybeth when she'd left for good. It took me a minute to pull myself together, but nothing could have prepared me for seeing Maya in the state she was in. I needed answers, but my anger was getting the best of me. Sending her to get cleaned up was the only way I could get some space. Did I want her to know I left her room as a shrine? Absolutely not, but I also needed a minute to get my head straight. Looking at her covered in blood and dirt was just too much.

"Anton?" her voice soothed me even after so much time had passed.

"Do you feel better?"

She must have showered. Her dark hair was still wet, and she had a butterfly Band-Aid over the cut on her eyebrow. She looked better than before, but the bruising on her face was getting worse as time went on.

"I do."

"Sit down. I'll get some ice for your eye."

"It's fine."

"It's not fine, Maya, stop insisting everything is fine."

She took a seat across from my desk as I stood and went to the wet bar, pulling ice from the icemaker and wrapping it in a towel.

"Here, hold this to your face."

"Thanks."

I moved around my desk and took my seat. Looking at the woman who broke me as badly as I broke her was harder than I thought. She drove me insane, and I did the same to her. It was who we were until it all became too much.

"Start from the beginning."

"I was on a job and, like I said, the guy got violent. He's pushed me before, but never like this. That night he was insane, so I did what I needed to do to protect myself."

"Not there. The real beginning. How did you end up leaving me and running to Tommy Marconi?"

Maya shook her head, and I thought she was going to shut down, but finally she looked up at me with the fire in her eyes I remembered and started talking.

"I didn't go straight to Tommy. You told me to leave, and I tried to do that. I took a bus out to my cousin's place but things didn't work out there, so I came back. I was working night shifts at a diner and Tommy's girls used to come in. It's not a bad job, Anton; the job isn't what got me in trouble. It was one man."

"The job isn't what got you in trouble? Maya, if you weren't fucking the asshole, then this never would have happened." I couldn't keep from yelling and the fact that she flinched as if I would hit her made me sick. God knows what she had been through since she left me. I knew she went to her cousin's and once I found out she was working at the ranch, I breathed a little easier. I thought she would be okay there. Maybe she could move on.

"I don't need you to lecture me, Anton. I came here because I've run out of options. Tommy's been after me since the night everything happened, and I can't keep hiding around the city. I need to work."

"Wait a minute, who did this to you?" I said, pointing at her battered face.

"Two of Tommy's goons. He's been sending them after me for weeks now, but today I couldn't get away."

"You're telling me the guy that you killed didn't do this to you?"

"No. That was three weeks ago."

"Three weeks? Three weeks ago, you killed some fucking asshole and you've been hiding ever since?"

"Yes, and I was doing fine until this afternoon."

"Why didn't you come to me then?"

"I didn't need you then!" She stood up and started pacing the office. I was so fucking pissed I couldn't even hear her. The ringing in my ears and the need to spill blood made everything a blurry mess.

"I wouldn't have needed you now, but Eddie caught me coming out of the clinic."

"Clinic? What clinic? Maya, what the hell is going on? I'm not going to ask you again. Tell me the whole fucking story."

She sat back down and started talking as I tried to control my breathing and calm the fuck down. My head felt as if it were going to explode.

"I go to the clinic every month to get tested. I'm not an idiot, Anton. I know there are risks with what I do."

"And?"

"And I'm clean, if you must know," she spat back, rolling her eyes at me, "When I killed that guy, Tommy lost his shit. He was a whale, one of his largest clients, and he threatened to sell me to make up for the money he'd lost. I wasn't going to let that happen, so I ran. I have no idea what happened after that. Things were quiet for a few days, but then I caught a couple of his guys tailing me. I moved around every night and thought I had lost them. It was dumb to go to the same clinic I always went to. I made a mistake and Eddie grabbed me when I was coming out. He threw me in a van and told me he was taking me back to Tommy. I beat his ass and got away."

"Eddie did this to you?"

"Yeah. But I got away."

"I'm going to kill him."

"They will never stop coming for me."

"Then I'll never stop killing them."

"That's not why I came here. I thought you could get me a new identity. Birth certificate, passport, the works. I know you're the best in the city. I'll pay you what I can, but it's not much. Once I get out of the country, I'll get a job and wire you more."

She had lost her mind if she thought I would let her ever leave this house again. "You aren't going anywhere."

"I'm not staying here. They will find me. Honestly, I'm surprised you haven't heard from him already."

"Tommy isn't a fool. He knows to keep his distance from me. But he made one big mistake, and that was you."

"What do you mean?"

"He should have never let you work for him. I'm not surprised he's been so quiet over the years. If he had you, then he wouldn't have wanted me to know."

"He's a dangerous man."

"Maybe, but only because he's crazy. If he thinks he can run shit like this in Dante's city, then he's going to end up with more than he asked for."

"You can't tell Dante."

"Why not?"

"Tommy will know he found out because of me. He'll kill me, Anton. I know he will."

"Maya, I don't think you understand. Tommy Marconi is a dead man. No one lays a hand on you. No one. I'll fucking kill all of them. The world will bleed for what they did to you. You are done with this life you built yourself. If you want my help, then you will do what I say. That mouth of yours has gotten you in trouble before, and it will again. Do you understand me?"

I watched as she fidgeted in her seat. Maya never liked being told what to do. The only time I could get her to comply over the years was in the bedroom, and even then, her bratty nature always got her punished. Our relationship was toxic. Fight, fuck, make up. I tattooed the shit on my forearm so I'd never forget what she put me through. What we put each other through.

"I understand," she whispered without looking at me.

"Go to bed. I'll send Marybeth in with your tea."

"You still keep it?"

"I kept everything of yours, Maya. This is your home."

She stood and turned from the room. My heart ached so badly I rubbed my chest to relieve the pain. I picked up my phone and texted Marybeth, just as I had done earlier. This time, instead of medical supplies, I asked her to bring Maya dinner and the mint tea she loved. It was late, but she wouldn't mind. The old woman was heartbroken when Maya left and never came back. Maybe even as much as I was.

After that, I picked up the phone and dialed the one person I'd been avoiding for the last six months.

"Isn't it a little late to be calling?" Dante Corsetti's voice came over the line.

"I have a problem."

"You don't work for me, remember?"

"I'm not calling you for help. I'm just calling with information."

"And that is?"

"I'm going to kill Tommy Marconi."

"You sure about that? Tommy isn't that easy to kill."

"I'm very... motivated."

"Maya?"

"Did you know?"

"I did."

Asking the Don of the largest crime family to explain himself was something that was frowned upon, but I couldn't help myself. Dante may be in charge of things now, but we still grew up together, and it gave me more leeway than others.

"How long?"

"Since the night she started with him."

"Why didn't you say anything?"

"She wasn't yours Anton, you let her go, and she chose her path. What did Tommy do to her?"

"He's been after her for weeks. She showed up here tonight beat to hell by Eddie and looking for a passport."

"Did you give her one?"

"No, and she's not getting one either. I'm going to stop this fucking madness before it gets any worse."

"You and Tommy go back pretty far. Are you sure about all this?"

"He's a piece of shit, Dante, you know that. I don't give a fuck what his father did for my mother's family. I'm not part of the Bravata, just like I'm not part of your family. My parents both died at the hands of killers, people they knew and trusted. I'd rather not go out that way."

"If you accepted my offer, we would handle this for you."

"That life isn't for me anymore."

"Says the man who called me just to tell me he was planning to murder two men instead of forging documents for his woman to run."

Fuck off was at the tip of my tongue, but I knew better. "This is different."

"Is there anything else?"

"Did you know he was trafficking?"

"It's not been confirmed, only rumors."

"It's confirmed now. He wanted to sell her."

"I appreciate the call. If anything changes, get back in touch."

The line went dead. My father spent years working for Dante's father. Then the two of them were shot down in cold blood and the whole world turned upside down. My mother was the daughter of the Russian mob boss, and the marriage between the two families kept everyone at peace for so many years. Now, with both of them dead and me being the only surviving heir, I spent more time turning down the Bravata and the Corsetti families' offers than I did anything else. Dante was a good leader, but things were unsettled in the city. Underlings like Tommy kept trying to rise up the ranks, and Dante spent most of the time knocking them back down. If I took care of Tommy, it would solve Maya's problems and also help the Corsetti family. Two birds, one stone.

"Sir?"

I looked up and found Marybeth at the door. "Yes?"

"She's settled into bed. I made her take a few bites of food, but she's exhausted and couldn't get much down. She is nauseous and has a terrible headache and I'm worried she may have a concussion. Would you like me to stay with her?"

"No, it's okay. I'll keep an eye on her through the night."

"Okay. Good night then."

"Goodnight."

I turned off my computer and picked up my phone before leaving my office, and made my way over to the other side of the house. It would have been hard enough with Maya sleeping in the next room. Watching over her while she slept was going to be one of the hardest things I had done in a very long time.

CHAPTER THREE
MAYA

I dreamed of blood. Blood on my hands, on the floor, in the bed. No one tells you how much a man bleeds when you stab them. The blood haunted me, made me question my sanity. I'd be going through my day without a care in the world, then I'd look down and see blood on my hands. It was everywhere that night. Going to the police wasn't an option. Tommy took care of it all. I just didn't realize how much it would cost me.

After waking up again, I rolled over in bed. I was restless and kept feeling as if I was being watched. I'd heard Anton go into his room a while ago, and then he opened the connecting door between our two bedrooms. When he didn't come in, I tried to go back to sleep. My head hurt worse than anything I'd felt before and if I moved too quickly I'd get a sharp pain in my side. I pushed myself up carefully and let out a gasp.

"What are you doing in here?"

"Marybeth was worried about you. I told her I'd keep an eye on things so she could sleep."

"How long have you been sitting there?"

Anton picked up his phone that had been sitting on the arm of the chair. "About four hours."

"I told you both I was fine, you should go to bed."

He stood and crossed the room, coming towards me. "Where else did he hurt you?"

"It's fine Anton, really I'm okay."

"Lay back, Maya." His hand came up and held the un-injured side of my face. I couldn't help myself. As much as I hated doing it, I melted into his touch as he gently pushed me back onto the pillows. When he pulled his warm hand away, an uncontrollable whimper escaped me. I missed Anton with every fiber of my being and now with him looking down at me, I never wanted this moment to end. He was my safe place. Always was, always would be. He was the little boy who brought me to his mother when we were kids and told her about my bruises. He told her what my father did to me and I never left. That was the first time he saved me. Little did I know it wouldn't be the last.

He turned on the light and then his hands reached for my shirt. Even the fabric running over my skin as he lifted it hurt. I tried not to squirm or make a face. If he knew how bad it was, he would just get angry again. I underestimated what I must have looked like. He gritted his teeth but didn't say a thing. Instead, he looked over at me, taking in every scratch and bruise he could find. He helped me sit up and removed my shirt, then my pants. I laid there in nothing more than a pair of panties, but it didn't bother me. Anton had seen my body a million times before this and even though I was bruised and battered, the heat rose between us like a tension rod ready to snap.

I lay still as he ran his hands over me, careful to avoid my ribs. He lifted my leg and kissed the inside of my knee that was scraped, and then my arm where the bruises from Eddie's grip were present. I was a mess and now he could see it all. When he was done with his inspection, his hands rested on either side of me.

"You should have told me. Your injuries are severe, Maya. Marybeth was right. I should have called the doctor for you earlier."

"It looks worse than it is."

"Every time you move in your sleep, you let out a cry. You don't need to keep pretending, not with me."

Tears welled in my eyes, so I looked away. I hated looking weak in front of him. I hated needing anyone's help. Anton was always my only exception. He was the only person who knew the real me. I felt his touch as he turned my face to him, then wiped away the tears. He leaned forward and placed a gentle kiss on my lips that felt like fire burning between us. When he pulled away, he helped me back into the shirt I had been sleeping in, covered me with blankets, and left the room.

I lay there wondering what the hell I was going to do now. I was weak under his spell and I needed to be strong. My strength and resilience were the only things that kept me alive. I made one mistake and got caught. But was it the only one? Or was coming here to Anton another mistake altogether?

"Here, take these," he said when he came back. He held out two white tablets and a glass of water, and I did as he asked. Whatever it was, it had to be better than the pain I was in. When I finished, he took the glass from me and set it on the table. Instead of turning to his room, he walked around the other side of the bed, removed his t-shirt and slid in next to me. He reached out as he had a million times before, and I slipped carefully into his arms. He let me adjust until I found a comfortable place. Laying on my side with my head in the crook of his arm was the most comfortable place in the world. His arm came around me gently and he placed a kiss on top of my head.

"Good night, Maya."

"Anton?"

"Yeah."

"Do you hate me?"

"No, get some sleep."

"I don't think I can."

"The pills will help with the pain."

"It's not the pain, it's the dreams."

"Did you talk to anyone after it happened?"

"No. How could I? I called Tommy and ran. The police would have thrown me in jail. My profession isn't exactly legal, and I had just murdered a guy."

"Why didn't you call me?"

That was one of the million questions I hoped I would never have to answer. The more time I spent at Anton's, the more he would dig into the mess my life had become since I left. How was I supposed to explain to him that if I called him, then it would be like nothing had ever changed? Three years later and I hadn't moved on. Calling him to fly in on his high horse and save me was proof of that. But so was coming to him tonight.

"I'm sorry I showed up like I did tonight."

"You didn't answer me. Why didn't you call me when everything happened?"

"I'm not your problem anymore."

"You were never my problem before, either. I've spent most of my life trying to convince you that you aren't a burden and you still don't believe me."

"It's hard to undo years of damage. You know that."

His silence was all the answer I needed. Laying in his arms was my favorite place in the world. I missed his embrace as much as I missed him. Our lives weren't fair in the way things turned out. For the longest time, we only had each other. Sure, adults were always around as we were growing up, but we did our best to stay out from under everyone's feet. Anton's family was dangerous and mine wasn't much better. As kids, we would lie in his yard just like this and stare up at the stars. We would make wishes and tell stories about how amazing our lives would be when we got older. Little did we know those moments were some of the best memories we would ever make. I loved Anton so fiercely it hurt. The lines between love and hate blurred so often with the two of us, I would forget what it was like not to have him in my life. We filled our lives with love, lust, and hate. It's all we knew. Then he told me to leave, and I did. I had left before but I always came back. That last time I didn't. I wanted to prove to myself I didn't need him. Day after day, I was miserable without him and there was nothing I could do about it. Something about that last fight felt final and now laying next to him, my body was burning for things it couldn't have. While my heart burned for a future I had lost.

I didn't realize I was crying until I felt the dampness between the side of my face and his chest. His arm tightened around me and he ran his large hand up and down my back. The movement was meant to calm me, but only made things harder.

"Look at me, little wolf."

I let out a breath I didn't know I was holding as I lifted my chin and stared up at the love of my life.

"I will fix this."

I wanted to ask what? Did he mean the situation with Tommy? Or us? My heart raced at the thought of either. If I were honest with myself, then I'd admit in the back of my mind I prayed tonight would turn out as it was. Anton wasn't my knight in shining armor, he was my wolf, like I was his. We were a fated pair, that's what he always said. He'd kill to protect me; he'd done it before and we were only children. There was no doubt he'd do it again.

Everything seemed to move in slow motion. His hand came up under my chin as his lips met mine. I shifted to get closer to him. Not an inch of space separated the two of us at that moment. My hips rolled forward on their own accord, pressing my heated center into him.

"Fuck," he ground out as his tongue darted in and out of my mouth. He was so careful, so gentle, it didn't even seem like him. Sex between us was intense, violent even, but something was different tonight. Something had shifted.

Anton's arm reached behind me and grabbed my ass, pulling me tighter to him. I pushed up and pulled my body over his, trying not to wince with the pain in my ribs. I straddled him and ground my pussy into his thick hard cock. I wished more than anything the clothes between us were gone. I leaned over him, kissing a line from the curve of his neck to his ear, and bit down hard when I reached his earlobe. His grip tightened, and he thrust upward with a growl.

"Little wolf, you are starting something you can't finish."

"That's not true," I whispered in his ear before tracing the shell of his ear with my tongue, "I can do anything I put my mind to. You're the one who taught me that."

His hands came up under my shirt and I lifted my arms over my head as he removed it. A chill came over me as he ran his fingers along the delicate tattoo that stretched under my cleavage. Memories of the night he took me to Ares' shop flooded my mind. The pain of the needle combined with him holding me was intoxicating. It was against every rule in the shop, but they allowed me to lie in his arms while the artist worked. The entire time, Anton's hands caressed my body, training it to love the pain as much as his touch. Every other tattoo I had was given to me by the same artist in the same shop, with Anton holding me. It paid off to have grown up with the shop owner.

I closed my eyes as he lifted his head and captured my nipple. He was sucking and pulling with his fingers on one side and his mouth on the other as I ran my hands through his hair, holding him to me. My thin leggings I put on after showering were no match for Anton. The friction of his hard cock against my clit as I rocked my hips back and forth reminded me of us as teenagers, learning each other's bodies, too scared to undress at first. It was hot, and I was close, too close to coming undone, and we hadn't even started. I slowed my movements and looked down at the beautiful man who held me. If only we weren't so toxic, if only things weren't so complicated, we could have this forever.

"Tell me what you need," he whispered into the darkness as his fingers slipped from my breast and down to the waist of my pants. He ran one finger along my skin, as if the need to torture me was more entertaining than the slickness between my legs.

"I need this," I said as I shifted back and lowered my hands to him, pulling at his gray sweatpants in an effort to release him.

"All you need to do is beg nicely, little wolf."

"Fuck me, please. I need you to fill me."

"Is your needy little cunt throbbing for me?"

"Yes."

"And if I run my finger between your folds, what will I find?"

"My warm, wet center."

"And whose little pussy is this?"

"Yours."

"Are you sure about that?"

"Yes."

"But it hasn't been only mine, has it?"

My heart stopped, and I froze. I hadn't been his, not in a long time. I'd given what was his away to others for the last three years. It was impossibly hard at first, but eventually I learned to ignore the feeling of disgust that crept up any time another man put his hands on me. Now I had to face that reality, and the reality that as much as Anton's body may want me again, his heart may never forgive me.

"I've always belonged to you, no matter what I did in the past. The only person who owns me, who owns my heart, is you," I choked out while trying to hold my emotions at bay.

"When you heal, you'll be punished for what you've done," he said through gritted teeth. I gave him a small nod, and he seemed pleased as he worked to remove the clothes we both had left. I knew it wasn't over, but we moved past the first hurdle we had to face.

Anton leaned back against the headboard and reached for me. I climbed back onto him, now with nothing between us, and he carefully helped me as I lined my body up perfectly with his. It had been so long since the two of us came together, but I knew his body better than I knew my own. I pushed myself up on his chest and lifted my hips as he lined himself up with my opening.

"Careful, little wolf. If you hurt yourself further, I will not be pleased."

His praise was what I lived for, and he knew that. The mind games we played with each other worked even in the most intimate settings.

I was slick with need, which made his entrance smooth. As I slid down his shaft, his hands tightened on my hips to an almost painful grip. I bit my lower lip and sighed as he finally filled me completely, staring up into my eyes. The connection between us shook my core in more ways than one.

I watched as a small smile quirked up his beautiful face. "Are you going to move, little wolf?"

I smiled back at him, not even realizing I stopped. Anton pulled me in as he always did, causing everything else around us to still and I shifted forward, lifting my hips slightly and coming back down in one smooth motion.

His sexy-as-fuck grunt was music to my ears.

"That's a good girl, just like that."

Lasting long wasn't an option. I was already on edge as I moved my body, sliding up and down again and again. When he caught my breast in his mouth, I nearly saw stars. He bit down and it only heightened my need for him. The pain in my body was nothing but a distant memory as I became consumed by the man I'd loved for my entire life.

"Fuck, Anton. Yes. More."

He fucked me from below as I begged and rocked forward and back, grinding my clit into him. His hips rose upward, and I gasped as he hit that soft spot deep within me. The whole thing made me want to explode and made the ability to hold off nearly impossible.

"Not yet, little wolf. Be patient."

"I can't wait. I need to —"

"You will wait. Do not come, Maya," he grunted out as he continued his movements, holding my lower back with one hand, pressing us tightly to each other, making me want to scream. Edging was one of his favorite games. Whether he tortured me with toys, his mouth or his cock, Anton never let me come without permission, sometimes holding out on me for hours or days if my behavior was unacceptable. It was one of his favorite punishments, but tonight was so much harder than before. It had been too long since I had him deep within me. My core clenched in pain as I mentally prepared myself for what was about to happen. Counting in my head and trying my best to concentrate on anything other than the sweet feeling building inside me was the only thing getting me through.

When his hand snaked between us and he slid his fingers to where we were connected, I almost lost it. He was toying with me. Playing my body as if I was his own instrument of pleasure. I tried my hardest to keep up with his movements, circling my hips to press my clit into his slippery fingers, but it was useless. I had to wait until he was ready.

"Do you need release, little wolf?"

"Yes."

"Beg."

"Please, please let me come. I can't wait anymore. It hurts too much. I need this. I need you."

A sly smile came over his face as I begged for release and then, without warning, he provided me the permission I craved and the dam that was holding me back burst into a million pieces. I screamed his name as he bit my neck and pinched my clit so hard I thought I'd die. The waves of my climax floored me and I shook over him as he exploded inside of me, coating my insides with his warm, slick arousal. The roar of pleasure that came from him vibrated within my chest and I collapsed, unable to move as the walls of my center pulsed around him, pulling into me every last drop he offered.

CHAPTER FOUR
ANTON

I couldn't sleep, but instead spent the rest of the night staring at the woman in my arms. The same woman who was now screaming like a maniac through the locked door of her room. I slipped from Maya's bed early in the morning and secured the doors between our two rooms and the door to the hallway. There was no way I was going to risk her leaving while I took care of things today. It wasn't even six yet, and she was already losing her mind. I sat on the edge of my bed after showering and heard her pull first at the door to my room, then at the one that enters the hallway. The scream of frustration that followed would have been comical if it wasn't so desperate. She had been alternating banging on each door and cursing me out for nearly an hour. Which made me thankful Marybeth's quarters were on the other side of my property. She was used to the chaos that ensued between the two of us, but the look of judgement over locking Maya away wasn't something I was in the mood for that early in the day.

I stood at the connected door when she had finally quieted down.

"Are you done?"

"Fuck you!" she yelled out, which only made me laugh.

"You will calm down before you hurt yourself. Do you understand me?"

"You can't keep me locked in here! Let me out, you pompous asshole."

"Name calling has never won you any favors, little wolf."

"Don't call me that. Just let me out of here. I want to leave. I don't want your fucking help anymore."

"No."

"Please Anton, I can't stay here," she said in a quiet voice that I knew all too well. It was her, 'let me act sweet and innocent to gain trust before I pounce' voice. I loved it when we played out a scene, but this morning it grated on my nerves.

"You will stay here Maya, and you will do so quietly."

I listened as she moved through the room. Suddenly, the door I was leaning on shook and glass crashed on the other side of it.

"Fuck off!" she yelled one final time.

"I am leaving. You will behave yourself for Marybeth today, and before you ask, she is not allowed to let you out of this room. She will bring you meals and your pills, but that's it. Now clean up that mess in there before you cut yourself."

I walked to my nightstand and picked up a burner phone, cash, and my guns. I doubt today would result in me being able to put a bullet through Tommy Marconi's forehead, but if I was lucky, maybe I could take out a few of his guys. They all deserved to die for what they did to my wolf, and I'd happily take each and every one of them out. It had been a while since I did this kind of work. Over the years, I'd call in favors to those who owed my family. Between my mother's connections and the work my father did for the Corsetti's, there were more than enough people in the city to do the dirty work for me. This was different, though. This time they fucked with me personally and that I wouldn't stand for.

I made my way down to the kitchen and found Marybeth already dressed and making breakfast.

"Early morning, sir?"

"There are some things I need to take care of today."

"And Maya?"

"Don't let her tantrum bother you. She knows the rules. I will let her out of her room when I get home. She has everything she needs there to rest and heal, although she's not pleased with it. Make sure you bring her food, and I left some pills on the vanity of my nightstand. She should take two every four hours for pain."

"And if she doesn't?"

"She will."

An hour later, I pulled up to my club and found Nico Marchesi already parked out front. Nico is completely unhinged, unpredictable, and Don Corsetti's right-hand man. If I said it surprised me to see him, that would be a lie. I knew Dante would stick his nose into this mess when I called him, but not calling would have been worse.

"You lost?"

"Nah. I'm right where I'm supposed to be."

"A bit early for a house call."

"It's a good thing this shithole isn't a house."

"Watch yourself, Nico."

He smiled, continuing to flip around a shining dagger in his hand. "You know why I'm here?"

"I'm not an idiot."

"You are if you think going after Tommy on your own is a good idea."

"Who said I'd be on my own?"

"Well, I don't see anyone else here at seven fucking a.m., do you?"

I didn't bother responding, but walked past him and unlocked the door. The club was huge, not as big as some of the Corsetti's places, but more than what I needed to pay the bills. I flipped the lights on as I made my way through to my office. Even after the cleaning crew came through the night before, it still held the faint smell of spilled liquor. I made a mental note to look for a new company. I pushed the door open to my office and took a seat, powering up my computer.

"How is she?" Nico asked once he found himself a place to sit on the couch in the corner.

"Fucking pissed."

"At Tommy?"

"At me. I locked her in her room this morning and left to the chorus of her screams."

"She's going to fucking kill you, bro."

"Nah, she knows better."

"I've known you and Maya my whole life, and to be honest, she's scarier than you are when she's pissed off."

"Ha. Ha."

"What did she have to say about Tommy?"

"Not much. I was so fucking pissed at her I spent most of the night arguing and the rest of it fucking her. She seems scared. It's not like her. He told her he was going to sell her."

"Fucking dick. I knew he was into some shady shit with the Romano's."

"The Romano's? Valentina's family?"

"Yeah, her cousin wanted us to get into trafficking. It's easy money, but Dante refused. He's been causing problems ever since. We got word Tommy was spending time over there."

"That's why Dante sent you?"

"No. He just didn't want you dealing with this alone."

"This doesn't change things. I'm not going to work for the family."

Nico sat there and said nothing. The smug look on his face made me want to get up and punch him, but unless I planned to die, that wasn't a good idea. Nico was the one who thrived in making people disappear for the Corsetti family. He also had a temper that was out of control and a thirst for blood. I've seen him turn into a rabid animal when his inner beast takes over, and poking that monster wasn't in my best interests.

"What's your plan?"

"I'm going to kill him, but I'm starting with the fuckers that beat the shit out of my wolf."

Sometime later, Nico and I were pulling up to a run-down warehouse in the meat-packing district. Tommy's father had owned it years ago, and now he ran his business from there. If you could call prostitution a business, that is. I have always found it entertaining how every kid of a crime family that I met when I was younger said they wouldn't do what their fathers did. Now, years later, we were all here doing the same shit. Each family had their own business, some more legit than others, and the next generation was busy hustling to keep things in order. I didn't envy Dante. Their business stretched far beyond New York City and the problems that arose were one nightmare after another. Most of us knew our place, but every once in a while some loud motherfucker would try to dethrone the king. It was pointless, really. Dante, Nico and Ares weren't known as The Dark Kings for nothing. Each of them was completely fucked in their own way and once you crossed them or those they loved, you didn't live to tell the tale.

"I take it you aren't going for a surprise visit?" Nico laughed as I pulled my SUV up to the front and laid on the horn.

"I'd rather them come out shooting," I said with a laugh as we got out.

"Fuck yeah, let's go hunting."

I pulled out both of my guns and held them up to the door. Nico preferred his knives, but his shoulder holster held two Berettas.

"Ring, ring, motherfuckers," I said, staring up at the security cameras.

It didn't take long for me to hear the locked door click, indicating it would open when I pulled the handle. I secured one of my guns and opened it, stepping through with Nico not far behind me. The warehouse was dark with two large shipping containers inside. It smelled like a combination of motor oil and piss, which caused me to crinkle my nose up as soon as we moved forward.

"Come out, come out where ever you are," Nico sang out, causing an echo that made my skin crawl.

The movement near the back office was intentional. Someone pushed a chair loudly along the cement floor, causing Nico and I to turn and see who the lucky winner would be.

"It's a bit early in the day, boys, but if you need some women, I can make some calls."

"I don't need your pussy, Eddie, we are just here to talk."

"Sure you are. If you wanted to talk, then you would have called. Instead, you are working your way through our building with loaded guns."

I came to a stop about five feet from the asshole and put my gun away. He'd die this morning, but not yet. I gestured for him to sit back down as Nico wandered around the warehouse. This wasn't his fight, and he knew it, but he'd enjoy himself just the same.

"Where's all your men?"

"Here, there. You know, around."

"Really? Because it looks pretty empty around here."

"Nico isn't the only one who creeps in the shadows. Are you here on Corsetti business? I heard you refused the Don's offer, but here you are, with one of his men."

"You know what I'm here for."

"Maybe you should enlighten me."

I walked around the back of his chair as I took a deep breath. I wanted to destroy this motherfucker, but I also needed to know where Tommy was.

"Where is he Eddie?"

"Who?"

"Cut the shit. I'm not in the mood today. We heard about Tommy's side gig and I'm ready to put it to an end."

"And here I was thinking you had come after me because of that slut, Maya."

I pulled the garrote from the clip on my belt and, in one quick movement, slipped it over his head and around his neck. Eddie's hands pulled at mine, scratching as he grunted for air. In the main part of the warehouse, I could hear a commotion. Nico was having a little fun.

"You don't get to say her name."

He choked and grunted a few more times before I let up the pressure. I needed to keep control until I found out where Tommy was hiding out.

"Where is he Eddie? I'm not going to ask again."

"Fine, fuck. He's been staying at the Waldorf."

I stood, releasing the wire completely, and walked around his desk as he lifted both hands to his neck, rubbing the deep red groove I left behind. He was too distracted by the need to regain his breath, so he didn't even notice when I pulled my gun.

"Street rats always turn quick," I said as I raised the gun, aimed and shot a bullet straight through his forehead, "That's for my wolf, motherfucker."

His body slumped over his desk and blood ran from the wound all over the papers he had in front of him. I couldn't help but smile at the mess it made. You fuck with my wolf and you die. It wasn't that hard to understand, yet people constantly tried me.

"All done in here?" Nico said as he walked through the office door covered in blood and dirt.

"How do you always get so filthy?" I asked as I secured my gun.

He smeared blood from his hands over his face and grinned. "It's a choice, not a side effect."

"Come on, I need to get back to Maya."

"Where's Tommy?"

"Holed up at the Waldorf Astoria."

"Fancy place for such a shit person."

"Yeah, that means business is a little too good for him. Maybe it's time we stop that."

CHAPTER FIVE
MAYA

Even though hours had gone by, it still pissed me off I was stuck in my room. Who the fuck did Anton think he was? He fucked me into submission and then locked me away. After he left, I spent the better part of an hour destroying anything I could get my hands on. Then the adrenaline wore off, and the pain came back. The day after a fight was always the worst. Not that I fought often, but over the last three years, I'd been beaten more times than I wanted to think about. Johns got pushy, sure, but it was Tommy's guys who were the worst. Then if I'd bruise, it would piss them off they couldn't get top dollar for me that night. Working the streets wasn't a bad thing, but the men who ran the business were.

Marybeth had been up a few times to check on me. I took the meds and ate the food she brought without argument. She wasn't the one I was mad at. That was Anton.

After I ate, I lay in bed with an ice pack she brought me and watched as she chatted away, cleaning up the disaster I created in my room. I tried to tell her I would take care of it, but as usual, she wouldn't listen. The woman was a saint, and it always made me wonder why she spent so many years working for Anton's family. She had been friends with his mother and the only thing that ever made sense was that she must have promised to look out for him. I dozed off for a while and then showered and changed. I still hurt everywhere, but I was beginning to feel like myself again.

I heard him the second he entered his room. His heavy footsteps were unmistakable, then the lock on the door clicked and they became distant, as he must have turned and walked away. I got up and walked to the door. The cold metal of the handle sent a shiver through my body as I turned it and pulled it open. My hesitance was unsettling. Anton was the one person in this world who knew me better than I knew myself, but there was something about the anger in his eyes last night that made me question my actions over the last few years. The shower was running and when I got to the door of the master bath, I stood there watching as the water ran over his muscular body. The tattoos he had all meant something to him. Many held memories, as did the scars that littered his body. Now he ran a nightclub and forged documents, but when we were in our early twenties, he got in more trouble than he needed to.

His arm came up, and he leaned forward, placing his forearm on the glass. His head rested against it as he reached for his thick cock and grasped it in his other hand. I was paralyzed as I stood there leaning on the door frame.

The gods themselves sculpted Anton. With long deliberate strokes, he moved his hand along his hard length again and again. My mouth watered and my pussy throbbed. My anger was quickly forgotten, and I wanted him. All of him.

"Are you lost, little wolf?" his husky voice floated to me as I looked up and found him staring at me with his piercing blue eyes. His light hair, eyes and skin were always a contrast to my darker features, and they drew me in like a moth to a flame.

I stepped forward into the bathroom as the steam enveloped me and pulled my clothes from my body as I went. The shower was a large glass enclosure with multiple showerheads, and it opened on either side. I always hated it because I never felt as if I could get it warm enough since the steam could escape, but at that moment I didn't care. I walked through the opening as he turned to face me. His hand never left its position as I kneeled in front of him and opened my mouth, asking for what I desired.

Anton's hand snaked around the back of my neck as he plunged himself down my throat. He wasn't a small man. The thickness that stretched my lips to a painful position rivaled his length. I choked and gagged as he fucked my mouth. The tears in my eyes burned, but the water washed them away.

"That's it, good girl," he groaned as I reached up and grasped the backs of his legs, pulling him to me as he moved.

"Fuck," he ground out through clenched teeth. Then his body tensed and he emptied himself into me.

He stepped back and turned into the water. I didn't dare move as he finished washing up. When he turned the faucet off, he looked down at me and a small smile came over him before he sealed it away.

"Make yourself presentable, Dr. Anders will be here within an hour."

He left the shower and dried off. I didn't stand until he went into the closet to get dressed. My heart hurt at the dismissal and my mind was raging war as it replayed my poor decisions. I should have never let my anger go. Stepping into this shower did nothing other than confirm for him where we both stood. Years ago, he would have taken care of me. Now I was left soaking wet on the floor of the shower and told to get myself ready. I don't know what I was expecting by joining him, but a cold shoulder wasn't it. I reached for a towel and patted myself dry so I wouldn't get water on the wood floors and made my way back into my room. When I reached for the door to close it behind me, I was stopped.

"Leave it open. I don't trust you anymore."

If I had thought of being dismissed like a school girl hurt, I was a fool. That was nothing compared to him telling me he didn't trust me.

The doctor was early. I had seen him in the past, so it didn't surprise me when he walked into my room.

"Maya, good to see you," he greeted me as he approached my bed with Anton on his heels.

"Good to see you too, Dr. Anders."

"Anton tells me you've had a bit of an accident."

"You could say that."

"Let's see what's going on, then."

Anton didn't even bother to pretend he would leave as the doctor began examining me. Instead, he sat in the chair

I found him in the night before with a look of fury as I was poked and prodded.

"I'm going to wrap your ribs before I go. I'm certain you have at least two that are severely bruised, but I don't think anything is broken. They will heal with time, but will continue to be painful until then. This should help," he said as he held up some ace bandages, "As for the cut on your eye, it's too late to stitch it. You will likely have a scar, but it doesn't look infected. I'm going to draw some blood, and I'd like you to take this to the restroom."

He held up a small white box, clearly labeled pregnancy test. "I'm not pregnant."

The doctor looked over at Anton instead of responding.

"Take the test, Maya."

"No. I'm not pissing on some stick just to prove I'm not knocked up."

"Yes, you will."

"You know what? This whole situation is bullshit," I said as I threw the box down next to me on the bed.

"Can you give us a minute?" Anton asked the doctor without ever moving his gaze from me. When the door closed behind Dr. Anders, he stood, picked up the box and grabbed a hold of my wrist, pulling me from the bed and into my bathroom. He threw the box down on the counter.

"Piss," he said pointing at the box.

"Fuck you."

"Maya, I'm not fucking around here. You will take that damn test."

"Or what?"

The second the words left my mouth, I knew I had gone too far. Anger flashed in his eyes as he grabbed my neck and held me up against the wall. I should have been angry, but the second he had me in position, the need to wrap my legs around him caused my pussy to throb and my mind turned to mush.

"Or you won't get what you want. You won't get me back, little wolf. My restrain and control is much better than yours. You will take the test so I know that womb is empty and ready for my seed. Do you understand me?"

I nodded the best I could. The memories of what we lost floated between us in a dense thickness that would have made it hard to believe, even if Anton didn't have his hand around my throat. Hurt and sadness crossed over his features and he let me go.

"Bring it to me when you're done."

I stood there shaking. Not from Anton's actions, but his words haunted me. The miscarriage that finally broke us seemed as if it were just yesterday, and now I was taking a pregnancy test in the same place I saw that first positive test all those years ago. I knew I wasn't pregnant, but there was no way Anton would believe me. So, with shaking hands, I unpacked the test, followed the instructions precisely, and walked with it back into the bedroom.

Anton and Dr. Anders were both there. The anger that radiated off the man I loved was overwhelming. Dr. Anders worked quickly as he drew my blood and wrapped my ribs. Anton sat quietly in the corner with the test in his hand as the doctor stood to leave.

"If you two need anything at all, I'm always available. Just call."

"Thank you," I said, as he left the room. I was exhausted and needed space, but the brooding asshole in the corner of my room hadn't left. With some difficulty, I pulled my shirt back over my head and laid down on my good side. If he wasn't going to leave, then so be it. I needed to sleep.

We sat in silence for what felt like an eternity before he finally broke the quiet.

"It's negative."

"I told you it would be."

"I needed to be sure."

I closed my eyes, praying he'd just leave, but I wasn't that lucky. I was never that lucky. "When this is over, we'll try again Maya."

Tears burned my eyes even though they were closed. I gasped for air as the pain shot through my chest. It's strange really how a person can feel their heart breaking a million times, yet it still beats and forces you to live. The bed dipped with his weight as he laid behind me and pulled me back to his chest. Anton nuzzled his nose into my hair and took a deep breath.

"You are my very own version of hell on earth, but you deserve everything you desire."

He ran his hand over my hip and lifted my leg over his, opening me up to him. The tears still hadn't stopped when he slipped his fingers inside of me. I felt his hard cock press against my ass while he plunged his fingers in and out of me. I pushed back into him and whimpered when he pulled his hand away.

"Suck them," he grunted out as he stuck them into my mouth, forcing me to taste my arousal, "So sweet," he purred before he made his way back to circle my clit. He didn't move quickly and didn't press hard. Just enough to raise my excitement, but not enough to injure me further. The gentleness Anton could display with my body always amazed me. His preference would always be so rough it was nearly violent and my need for that grew as well throughout the years.

"Come for me, little wolf."

I cried as his words tore the orgasm from me. Wave after wave of pleasure took over and all the sadness and anger I had felt throughout the day disappeared without a second thought. In that moment, everything was perfect and it would remain that way until I woke up hours later alone in bed, locked behind the thick wooden door.

CHAPTER SIX

ANTON

I t was nearly noon and not one of the assholes I lived with made their way into the main house yet. I was normally the first one up and the last one to sleep, but Ares and Nico were taking sleeping in to a whole new level. Yesterday was stressful for all of us and last night was even harder. I had imagined Valentina would fight us, refuse to stay, and make a scene. What I hadn't expected was for her to push anything Ares or I said about Nico to the side and crawl into bed with him. Seeing her with him both hurt and healed something deep inside me. I wanted her to myself last night. I wanted her under me, but I wasn't ready yet. Seeing her here in our home after finding her the way we did made everything too real. The guilt of leaving her in such a shitty situation for so many years was eating away at me.

The plan was for her to stay locked away in her room until she agreed willingly to stay. But after last night, I don't think her leaving was something we had to worry about. That didn't sit well with me. I needed to know why, and I was getting impatient. They had slept long enough. I made my way back to the bedrooms and opened Nico's door. There, lying in bed, were both Valentina and Ares. Fucking hell, that's not what I expected either. Jealousy sparked its ugly head and surprised me. We had shared women before, but seeing them with Valentina without me felt uncomfortable. She let out a soft sigh and I watched as her arms wrapped tighter around Nico's center before I had enough. I banged loudly on the door three times and laughed as I watched them all jump.

"Come on, the day is nearly over and we have shit to do," I said, continuing to enjoy their angry state. As Ares threw a pillow, I dodged it and saw the most adorable expression I had ever seen on Valentina's face. Nico cursed as I walked to the side of the bed and reached over him for her. I slid my hands under her arms and pulled her from the bed as if she were a small child.

"They have had you long enough. You are coming with me."

I walked from the room holding the most valuable thing in my entire world. I didn't want to like it as much as I did, but having her in my arms was making it difficult to tamp down the feelings swirling through me. Lust was all it was. It was all it was ever supposed to be. She would be my queen, the woman behind the men who ran the city, but I never planned for her to mean anything more than that to me.

"Where are you taking me?" she grumbled as she rubbed the sleep from her eyes.

When we reached the double doors of my master suite, I stepped inside and crossed the room to the bath. I placed her on her feet and closed the door behind me, instructing her to take care of whatever she needed and meet me back in my room. I needed sometime alone with her, time to understand what she was thinking, without the influence of the others.

She didn't take long and came right to me. I had her take a seat on the small couch in front of the fireplace and she tucked her legs under her in the most delicate way.

"Is there coffee in this place?"

"Yes, I'll have some brought up for you with breakfast."

Standing so close to her, having her here in my room, were fantasies of mine for so many years. Even looking at her, I couldn't believe she was there.

"Why now?" she asked, looking up at me.

"It was time."

"But they told me you'd come when I was eighteen. That was three years ago."

"There were complications after my father died."

"What kind of complications?"

"Promises were made and never kept."

"So you just left me there. Which brings me back to my first question. Why now?"

"Did you not want me to come?"

"I wanted you to come when I was younger. I wanted someone to come and take me from that place. They had prepared me to be your wife, even though I barely knew you. I knew what was required of me and I gave into it years ago, only to be let down when you decided you didn't want me anymore. Do you have any idea how hard it was to see you over the years and then be taken back to that place they kept me? To see you with other women knowing it could have been me, but I wasn't good enough?"

I knew I should have said something to make her feel better. I needed to tell her she was wrong, and that wasn't what happened, but my anger was clouding my judgement. She had been fed so many lies over the years. I was desperate to learn all of them. There was more information I needed. I needed to know why she hated her home so much and what really happened there.

"What was it like living there? You call it 'that place' and 'the place they kept me' rather than home. You refer to your father as a stranger and yet I should be the stranger to you."

She turned her eyes from mine and focused on pulling apart a throw pillow that was sitting next to her. I didn't move; I didn't breathe. I just stood and watched as she worked through what she wanted to share with me.

"It wasn't always terrible. I love my father even after everything he's done. I mean, he's my dad and the only person I've ever really had. My mother died when I was born, you probably already know that, but other than my cousin Mario, I don't have anyone else."

I cringed at the thought that her love for him would come between us, given what we did last night.

"Tell me about when it was terrible."

"It doesn't really matter anymore. You aren't sending me back there, are you?"

"There is no place to send you back to. The home you once knew was destroyed."

"What?"

"It's gone, Valentina. The house was cleaned and burned to the ground last night."

"My father?"

I ignored her question. Now wasn't the time. "What did he do to you to make you hate your childhood home?"

"You saw where he kept me. I wasn't always locked in there. Most of the time, I was allowed in my room or the main parts of the house. I could even go out on the grounds sometimes with a guard. He always told me it was for my own good. That I needed to learn to behave like a lady for you and follow rules. He would tell me if I couldn't keep my mouth shut, and learn respect, then you'd never come for me. Or if you did, you'd kill me for stepping out of line."

"And you believed that?"

"I did for a long time. Then I attended a family wedding, and you were there. Do you remember? It was my cousin Maria's wedding."

"I do."

"I watched you that night. You looked at me in a way that made me feel special. I saw how close you were with Nico and Ares and I couldn't imagine you being so ruthless that you would kill a woman you were supposed to marry. I asked my father's wife at the time and she called me naïve. She told me I was a fool to believe The Dark Kings wouldn't kill me for disrespecting them."

"Did you believe her?"

"Maybe. I guess so. Our lives are different from most people. Growing up with the families we had, the expectations were different. I never went to a real school or out to the mall with friends. I didn't have sleepovers or a boyfriend growing up. Anytime I asked why, or questioned his plans for me, he would have me removed and put back in my cell. So eventually I just stopped asking."

"But you were there last night."

"I was. It was the sixth night."

"Why?"

"He told me Angelo Costa was coming for me."

"You didn't want Angelo? Even after I never came for you?"

"No. I guess I still hoped you would come one day. But if I married Angelo, that would never happen."

There was a knock at the door and I opened it, allowing the staff from the kitchen to come in and set up breakfast for her. She reached for the coffee as soon as they left, but wouldn't look at me directly. I couldn't tell if she was afraid of me or if she regretted what she had shared.

"Valentina, I want to set a few things straight," I said as I took a seat at the small table she had sat at to eat. "Ares, Nico, and I are ruthless men. We have done horrible things in the name of protecting what is ours and we would do it all again. I was young but not a child when my father planned for our marriage. I knew the second I saw you that you would be mine, and I never doubted that, not once. The month you turned eighteen, my father was killed. I had a lot of responsibilities that I needed to focus on but that didn't mean I wasn't coming for you. The arrangement between our fathers was part of a much larger agreement and when you came of age, your father hid you from me rather than turning you over. It was the first of many infringements I would uncover."

"But I was there. I was always at that damn house. You could have come anytime, but you didn't." I could sense her irritation.

"You said it yourself, our lives are different from most people's. It's not like I could just knock on the door and tell him I wanted you. It took time to ensure you were really there and put together a plan to make things right again. My father kept journals of his business dealings and as I worked my way through them, I learned the history between our two families was extensive. I had many meetings with your father trying to negotiate new terms and, in the end, force was the only way to ensure the promises that were made would be kept."

"So now what? I mean, I don't think I understand everything that is going on here. What will my father say when he finds out I'm with you? What about Angelo? Will he come for me here?"

"No one will come for you here, Ragazzina. You are safe from others under our protection."

I watched as she picked up her coffee and took a careful sip. She looked like a small child with her hair up and in the clothes Ares had dressed her, but behind those eyes was a smart and calculating woman. She spent a majority of her life preparing for this moment and now that it had come, I needed to make sure it's what she really wanted. I wouldn't stand for a weak and pitiful woman with no thoughts of her own. Valentina would need to show us who she really is before I'd be willing to accept anything from her.

"Today you will stay in your room. I have business to take care of with Nico, so Ares will stay at the house with you."

"I can't leave my room?"

"No, not yet."

"So this is what it will be like, then? The same as it was before?"

"It will be nothing as it was before. This is your new life, Valentina, but before I open myself and my family to the risks of keeping you, you will need to decide that you want to stay."

"I want to stay. I don't want to go back."

"I already told you, there is no going back. Your house and the life you knew there is gone. It's over and it won't be the only thing you will lose. If you chose to stay, you will become one of us. The Romano name will no longer be yours. You will become a Corsetti, and with it, you will hold the responsibilities our name carries. You will fall in love with us all, and that will confuse you. We do not hide who we are. We will not hide ourselves from you. You get the good with the evil, but it's a choice I will allow you to make."

"And if I choose to leave, you will let me?"

"I will."

She sat there contemplating her next question carefully. I watched as she tilted her head slightly and gazed up at me. She failed at hiding the slight smile when she asked, "Who are you talking about when you say us?"

"You already know the answer to that question."

Valentina grew quiet. There wasn't much more to say right now. I respected that she asked nothing further. The rumors about the three of us and our relationships ran wild. I'm certain she knew what she was getting into. Her silence spoke wonders. Valentina Romano wasn't just some poor little girl that had been locked away for years. She was a queen in her own rights, and manipulation was her best skill for survival. I stood and went to her. As I lifted her chin, I leaned down and placed a gentle kiss on her lips.

"Fino a tardi, ragazzina. I will be back later this afternoon."

She looked like an angel when I pulled back. Her eyes were still closed and her lips were slightly parted. I wanted to ravage her in the best ways possible, but after learning she had never even dated before, it only confirmed my suspicions that she was a virgin. I needed to meet with Ares and Nico. We had to adjust our plans with her based on this new information. I wouldn't hurt her, but I also wouldn't deny myself what I had wanted and needed for so long.

I left my bedroom to find Nico stumbling out of his room and making his way to the kitchen.

"Morning sunshine."

"Fuck off."

"Where's Ares?"

"No idea. He left when you came in like an asshole and ruined the best moments of my life."

"The best moments were while you were asleep?"

"Lay with her tonight and you'll know what I mean." He looked behind me toward the closed door of my master. "Where is she?"

"Having breakfast in my room."

He went to turn, but I stopped him. "Not now. We have work to do. Angelo Costa is publicly mourning the death of his fiancée."

CHAPTER SEVEN
MAYA

My pussy was ruined. Anton was still hard inside me even after emptying himself, and I ached as he slowly slid out of me. Nothing and no one ever compared to him in bed. Our bodies were meant to be together, which is why I knew the only way to gain points was to offer myself to him. It wasn't a hardship, that's for sure. In the hours he'd leave the house, my heart felt empty. We were always inseparable, but now he forced me to stay here while he went on with life. It didn't feel right, and yelling wasn't getting me anywhere.

He turned me onto my back and undid the restraints, holding me to the spreader. I didn't have many toys in my room, but the few I had, I put to use. We kept our larger collection in Anton's side of the master. He rubbed my legs and hips once I was free, ensuring I didn't complain about any pains. The movement was familiar and made my heart flutter a little too fast. He did the same with my hands and once he was satisfied I wasn't hurt, he stood and picked up his clothes.

"Where are you going?"

"To shower, again."

That awful pain in my chest came back as it did often. Aftercare was the one part of playing Anton never skipped. Since I got back, this wasn't the first time he ensured I was good and then walked away. When we started this lifestyle, aftercare was uncomfortable for me. It took time for me to enjoy him bathing me, washing my hair and holding me for hours. But I had grown used to it and now, with it missing, it was clear we still weren't where we needed to be.

"Get dressed, we are going to the club," he said as he turned his back and walked to his room.

My disappointment at how he left me was quickly forgotten. I would have bounced out of bed and jumped for joy if I hadn't just been fucked into submission. That asshole did this on purpose. He could have denied me, left me be, screwed me quickly and went on his way, but no. He forced two earth-shattering orgasms on me in less than thirty minutes just to ensure I wouldn't be a problem for him tonight. My inner demon child laughed a sinister laugh inside my mind, but I knew this was all a test. Anton did nothing without calculated consideration, so if we were going out, it was to prove a point. I didn't know what that point was yet, but I'd find out soon.

I heard the water running in his bathroom. I slowly got to my feet and instead of heading to my bathroom, I went to his. The steam had overtaken the space, but I could easily see my way around. If he wasn't going to provide me with the aftercare I needed, then he didn't deserve alone time. I stepped into the open end of the shower and turned on one of the extra shower heads. Anton's back was to me as the water ran over him. His eyes were closed, but he knew I was there. The tension in his body was the telltale sign I was close to him. It was the same tension I had when he was around. The only cure to it was his touch. When we were connected, I was calm. When we weren't, my body felt as if it was going through withdrawal.

I reached for the soap and gently washed myself. It still hurt when I bent over, but the pain was manageable, if not enjoyable. For a lot of my life, pain was the only thing that made me feel alive, pain and Anton. When I slid my hands between my legs, I looked up and found his eyes on me. He hadn't told me to leave, but he also hadn't invited me. I lifted my other hand to my breast and pulled at my nipple, closing my eyes and tilting my head back to put on a show for the man that made me insane.

His movement was quick and before I realized what had happened, he pressed me up against the glass wall of the shower. Anton had a hold of my neck and I tilted my head to the side, smiling up at him.

"Can I help you?" I asked with a grin.

"Needy little whore," he grunted as he got to his knees, and lifted my right leg over his shoulder. His mouth was on me in record time, forcing a grunt from me as he pushed me harder into the wall. I held onto his head to steady myself as he attacked my clit and forced his fingers deep inside me. He was right. I was a needy little whore, I was his needy little whore. I couldn't tear my eyes away from him. His mouth covered my center, and he sucked and licked at my core until I shattered into a million pieces.

Anton lowered my leg and held me steady as he stood. I looked up at him with a shy smile, but he saw right through me. His lips crushed down on mine as he lifted me up against the wall and shoved his cock into my still pulsing center. It didn't take long, we climaxed together in record time. It shocked me he could pull anymore from me, but the second he slid home I was ready again. He fucked me hard and fast with anger in his eyes, and I held on for dear life as my nails pierced the skin of his shoulders. I screamed out his name as he growled his release and when it was over, he put me down, kissed my forehead, and washed my hair. I may not have gotten everything I wanted from him, but it was definitely a good start.

"What the fuck are you wearing?"

"Oh, this old thing?" I said as I twirled enough so that my already short skirt flipped up, showing off my ass.

"Get back in there and change your fucking clothes."

"No,"

"Do you want to try that again?"

"No. If you didn't want me to wear this, then you wouldn't have bought it."

Anton gritted his teeth and clenched his fists as he turned and wrenched open the door to the hallway. "Come on."

I followed close behind as we walked down the front steps and out to his Maserati. It was one of my favorite cars he owned and he knew it. As I approached the car, he opened the door like a perfect gentleman. The only thing amiss was his look of complete aggravation, and I loved it. He slammed the door closed and crossed in front of the car. He got in, started it up, and pulled down the long private drive without saying a word.

Taking matters into my own hands, I slipped my arm under his and placed it on his upper thigh. He didn't look, didn't flinch, nothing. It was almost as if I wasn't there at all.

"I was thinking... maybe if I behave for you tonight, I should get a reward."

"I'm absolutely certain you will not behave even if I agree to something like that."

"You never know. With the right motivation, I can often be persuaded into doing things I wouldn't normally do. But you already know that, don't you?" I let my hand slide to his already hardening cock. Even in his dress pants, I could feel him twitch with need.

"And if you don't behave, what will I get?"

"Anything you want."

"Anything?"

"Yes, anything."

"Will you sit in your fucking room and not be a nuisance until I kill Tommy? Because that's all I've asked of you, Maya, and you can't even seem to do that."

I pulled my hand away and crossed my arms over my chest. "You know what, Anton? I'm getting pretty sick of this fucking game."

"It's not a game. I told you what I needed from you the second you showed up. Tommy needs to die. When that's done, we can figure the rest of our shit out."

"The rest of our shit?"

"Yes, as in what the hell I'm going to do with you when this whole thing is over."

"You aren't going to do anything with me. I still want a passport. I still want to leave."

"Stop lying."

"It's not a lie!"

He pulled over to the side of the road and slammed on the brakes. The next thing I knew, he had me pressed up against the glass of the passenger's door.

"You don't get to leave Maya. Not now, not ever. You are mine, and I'm fucking over this mess of bullshit and lies."

He released his hold, and I reached for my neck as I watched him fix his jacket and put the car back into gear. "Don't fuck with me tonight, little wolf."

Those were the last few words he said to me until we arrived at the club.

Anton pulled up and got out, handing his keys to the club manager as he walked around my side, opened my door, and reached for my hand. I twisted my frame with my legs crossed and stepped from the vehicle and into an onslaught of people with cameras pointed in our direction. One of the greatest appeals of the Maserati was the eyes it drew in. The last thing I was going to do was show the world I had nothing on under this dress. That was for Anton's eyes only.

"Let's go," he said through the fake smile he had plastered on. The crowd parted, and we stepped into the club. It had been years since I walked through that door, but the sounds, the smells, and the lights felt as familiar as Anton had. My first job was working at this club and it wasn't until I was in my early twenties that I began stripping at his father's club. He was never a fan, but at the time he couldn't do anything about it either.

With his hand on my back, he had pulled me into his side, guarding me from the drunken patrons on the dance floor. There was a separate entrance we used during the day and some nights when he wanted to sneak in unseen, but tonight was a night that the owner of the club wanted the world to know he was there. We reached the back bar and went upstairs to the balcony that looked over the entire place. Dancers on large speakers circled their hips to the music and the men below couldn't keep their eyes off of them. I missed that rush of adrenaline that accompanied performing. I hadn't been on stage since the club shut down and for the longest time, dancing was a huge part of my life.

Anton came to a stop and pressed his body against mine up against the railing. His right hand came up, and he turned my head to the cage I used to dance in. A young girl no older than twenty was in it and she was having the time of her life.

"I miss watching you. This place isn't the same since you left," he said as he pressed his hips into my backside. "One day, when I can trust you won't run on me, I'll bring you back here, shut everything down and watch as you dance for only me."

My body melted into his. The image of me looking down at him while I danced naked in the cage shot through my mind as he ran his hands over my body.

"Now come, I have business to attend to tonight."

Anton took my hand, and we moved to the private room in the back. As we stepped inside, ten guys greeted him, three of which we knew since we were kids. Dante Corsetti, Nico Marchesi, and Ares Sabino didn't stand, but instead nodded their heads in our direction. It wasn't lost on me that there wasn't another woman in the room other than the ones who worked for the club. Some were serving drinks, another had a tray of white powder, and there were two in the laps of both Nico and Ares. I watched as Ares' hand disappeared into the top of the woman's dress and she sucked on his neck. The look on his face was one of annoyance, not enjoyment.

"Good to see you all," Anton said as we took a seat across from them.

"You can cut the shit Anton, I know you're not pleased we are here."

"I'm assuming it's for something important."

Dante tilted his head to Ares.

"Everyone out. Go jerk off in a corner," Ares shouted with a laugh as the room emptied.

"We could have met in my office."

"I like it here," Dante answered.

"The Romano's have become more trouble than they are worth. Something needs to be done about it, but I can't move until you settle your score with Tommy."

Anton held his hand out, and I moved to sit in his lap. "What he did to Maya is unforgiveable."

"I agree. But this is holding up other... things that need to be settled."

"The auctions?"

"That and more. There was a promise made to my father by Mr. Romano that has not been fulfilled. I intend to collect that debt, and soon."

"Have you had any luck tracking him down?" Anton asked Ares as his hand gripped my hip tighter than before.

"No. A bunch of dead ends. But he'll surface."

"So, what do you want me to do?"

"The way I see it, you have two choices. Agree to work for the Corsetti family and continue to pursue Tommy with our help, or you leave until what I need to do is finished. Then you can come back and deal with Tommy. If he's still alive, that is."

"You want me to run?"

"Consider it as going into hiding. Lying low if you like, but you and Maya need to leave town."

I wanted to say something, anything, to help the situation, but that they were even speaking in front of me was an exception to every rule. I bit my lip and held my breath as Anton leaned back in his chair, pulling his hands from me. All three men were staring at him. The only noise in the room was the muffled sounds from the music of the club and the slight scrapping noise Nico's dagger made whenever he flipped it between his middle and index fingers. He wore huge silver skull rings that caused the noise as the dagger dragged over them.

"You want the club?"

"No. We have our own. You'll continue to run yours along with your... other... business. Considering we already buy all of our documents from you, that won't change. We will work out protection for payment, and you will have a seat at my table."

I didn't know much, but Dante was offering Anton an awful lot, considering our situation. Well, my situation that I pulled Anton into. The guilt was eating me alive. I had always known his feelings about working for the Corsetti's and now, because of my mistakes, his hand was being forced. I turned to look at him but couldn't tell which way he was leaning.

Dante stood, and Nico and Ares followed. "You have until tomorrow to decide. I tried to wait until we settled everything, but this is taking too long and I've had to move up the job I need to get done. I've known you nearly as long as I've been alive, Anton, I won't fuck you the way my father fucked yours. We aren't those men, we are the new regime and I get to make the rules now."

Anton stood and shook hands with all three of them. They left, and the others made their way back into the private room. Anton took Dante's seat in the corner and motioned for the waitress to bring him a drink and me a bottle of water. I didn't have it in me to argue for something stronger. He looked defeated and I knew it was all my fault.

CHAPTER EIGHT
ANTON

"We should talk about this," Maya whispered into my ear. I didn't bother to respond. I had nothing to say to her. She pulled back when the waitress showed up and handed me my drink. Whiskey, neat, and it went down way too easily. Maya shifted in her seat. The assholes in our room couldn't take their eyes off her and it had me on edge. I felt her small hand on my thigh. Normally it would be comforting, but right now I want nothing more than to punish the fuck out of her for the position she'd put me in.

"Anton, please," she whispered again. I grabbed her wrist and pulled her hand from me.

"Stop, Maya."

"No, we need to talk about this."

"This offer has nothing to do with you," I ground out between clenched teeth.

"This has everything to do with me," she snapped.

I looked past her, trying my hardest not to let her get to me. She was dangling an argument, and I was already pissed. She never knew when to just leave something alone, and by the look on her face, I realized she wasn't pleased with being told no.

"Know your place, Maya."

The second the words left my mouth, I knew I'd made a mistake. Nothing pissed her off more than being treated as less than my equal. I watched as she stood, then reached for the bottle of water in front of her. She removed the lid and took a sip. Then, like the little brat that she was, she turned, smiled like a heathen and dumped the entire thing into my lap. The men in the room went silent as she stared me down with her hands on her hips.

"You think you can ignore me?"

I stood up, grabbing her by the neck and tilting her head to the side as the room cleared out. "Don't you fucking talk to me like that, little wolf. Have you lost your mind?"

Her body twitched under my hold, and I knew she wanted desperately to argue with me. But I kept my grip tight. "I know you are pissed, but like you said, this has everything to do with you. It's all your fault I'm in this position, so you don't get to call the shots. You showed up after three years needing me, and now look where it got us."

I released her and watched as she stumbled backwards. "If you're well enough to fuck with me, then you're well enough to be punished. Get on your knees."

The fury building in me only increased as she looked behind her to make sure we were alone before she finally lowered her head and knelt.

"Very good. Now clean up the mess you've made."

She carefully reached for me, undoing my belt and pants. My cock was so fucking hard it hurt. When we were younger, I couldn't understand how her mouthing off to me was such a turn on. Eventually, I stopped questioning it. This was who we were. She challenged me and I fought back, again and again, until we broke.

When her tongue darted out and licked the pre-cum from my cock, I groaned in pleasure. There was no need to hide it from her. She knew the hold she had over me. Even when everything around us was going to shit, my world revolved around her. I grabbed the back of her head and gripped her hair when she opened her mouth to take me in. She may have thought she was in control at that moment, but she wasn't. I pushed forward and didn't stop until I heard her choking on my rock-hard shaft. I'd fuck her face until she cried, then walk her out of this club with her tear-streaked face and wrecked hair, so everyone knew she was my little whore and no one else's.

I pushed myself forward again, holding her head in place as she choked on my dick and stared up at me. A smile came over her face and I watched as her head bobbed in time with her sucking, pulling the anger from me in the only way she knew how.

"That's it, there's my good little wolf. You like that?"

She hummed her agreement, causing a vibration that shot straight to my balls.

"Very nice," I grunted out my approval, "You're going to suck my cock until I fucking explode into that dirty little mouth of yours. Then I'm going to take you home and deliver every one of the punishments you deserve. I've been keeping a list."

Maya's eyes rolled back into her head as she sucked harder and faster. When she reached for my balls and massaged them in her hand, I was done. I held her to me as I detonated into her mouth as she swallowed everything I had to give her. I pulled back from her slightly and without instruction she licked me clean, then leaned back on her heels, waiting for further instructions.

"Get up," I said as I put myself away and reached for her hand, "We're leaving."

As we walked through the club, I admired the woman by my side. She held her head high as I led her along with a hand on her back. She looked thoroughly ravaged. Her makeup was a wreck and her hair had come loose from the slicked back ponytail she had it in. She had never been more gorgeous. Once we got out to the car, I helped her in and leaned over to buckle her seatbelt. She reached for me and placed a gentle kiss on my lips. The softness her eyes shown in moments like these plagued me with memories of our first kisses when we were only children. The same memories that some days brought heartache and other days brought comfort.

"Thank you," she whispered when she let me go.

The ride home was quiet. She looked out the window in silence and I drove with nothing to say. We both knew what was coming. It was long overdue. Sure, I wanted her well enough to take me and I wasn't certain she was one hundred percent, but I couldn't wait anymore. Tonight was the night, and even though she would hate it, I had every intention of being careful with her.

We walked into the house, and I stopped her in the foyer. "Take your clothes off."

"Here?"

My anger spiked, and I raised an eyebrow in her direction, "Do you really want to question me, little wolf?"

"No, sir."

She grit her teeth and dropped her purse on the floor next to her. Next, she slipped out of her heels and then turned her back to me. "Would you mind?"

I reached for her zipper and slowly undid it. As it lowered down her back, I realized not only was she not wearing a bra, but she hadn't even bothered with panties. When it dropped from her body, she stepped out of it and turned with a sly smile on her face.

"You little vixen," I grunted out as I pressed her body up against the wall, caging her in, "You left this house with your pussy exposed."

"Yes, sir."

I undid my pants, then picked her up and impaled her against the wall as she cried out. She was hot and slick, ready for everything I had to give her that night.

"Your decisions tonight have caused you nothing but trouble. It makes me wonder if this was your plan all along. Drive me insane until I fuck the hell out of you," I growled into her ear as I punished her pussy for everything she had done.

"Tell me, little wolf... is your bark worse than your bite?"

She leaned her head forward, and the instant her teeth met my skin, I trembled. She had moved my dress shirt back and her hand ran over the tattoo of her name on my chest. I knew her heart better than I knew my own. She was mine. I decided in that moment it didn't matter what had happened before. I wasn't letting her go again.

I thrust into her harder and faster as she gripped my shoulders, holding herself up until she screamed out my name. Her body convulsed and shook while her cunt throbbed and I emptied myself into her. Maya's breathing slowed as I held her against the wall, taking deep breaths to prepare myself for what would come next.

"Now. Get on your knees and let me watch my cum drip from that pussy while you crawl to our room."

I let her go and helped her to the floor. Her body was still weak and shaking from her climax, but she followed instructions perfectly. In the back of my mind, I hoped Marybeth was sound asleep on her side of the house as I watched the love of my life crawl her way down the cold marble floors of the hallway. The sight of her pussy, wet and glistening as she moved, sent a chill through me. One of excitement and adoration. She got to the two doors of our bedrooms, passed hers and went straight into the master. By the time she got there, I could see the slickness between her thighs dripping down her towards her knees.

"Very good, little wolf. Wait here."

I ran my hand along her shoulders as I passed her and went to the master bath. I pulled my clothes off and cleaned myself up. Then I stepped into my closet and opened the locked cabinet that held everything I planned to use that evening. With my arms full of Maya's favorite toys, I walked back into the room and found her right where I left her. My girl may want to rival me in public, but when we were behind closed doors, she craved nothing more than my approval. I laid everything out and motioned for her to stand and come to me.

She followed me to the wall where I opened the two compartments that held her restraints. It's not like I had people in my room often, but the design of having them enclosed into cabinets flush with the wall wasn't something I could pass up. Marybeth knew enough about the two of us she wouldn't judge, but that didn't mean I wanted chains hanging from my bedroom walls at all times. The design was perfect and every time I glanced toward the enclosed cabinets, I would picture Maya tied up. It had been my own personal punishment for the last three years without her.

When we reached the wall, she stood in position. I opened the boxes and pulled the golden chains free, and attached the leather cuffs to both her wrists. Once she was where I wanted, I went to the end of the bed, where I left everything and grabbed the spreader. She moaned as I ran my hands down the back of her legs and cuffed her ankles to it so she couldn't move. With one look up, I could see the need in her eyes. Maya was nothing if not transparent.

"Why are you being punished tonight, little wolf?"

"For disrespecting you, sir."

"Remind me how you disrespected me."

"By throwing water on you, sir."

"No, little one, it's not the water. You paid your penance for that at the club. Tonight I will punish you for leaving me, and for letting other men have what's mine. Do you understand?"

She whimpered as I reached and twisted both of her nipples between my fingers. "Yes, sir."

I picked up the black layered paddle I knew she loved. There was something special about the sound it made that she just couldn't resist. Its sleek shape never gave me the satisfaction I desired, but it would work to warm her up. I pulled her hips forward, causing her to stumble, pulling the restraints around her wrists tighter. She grimaced at the pain, but before she could focus on it, I pulled my hand back and slapped her ass with the tip of the paddle. She shrieked and her body thrust forward, trying to escape the next slap. It was useless, though. From the position I had her in, I could do what I wanted, and she had nowhere to go. I would have preferred to have her over my lap, but I worried about the pressure that would place on her bruised ribs, so this was the best I could do for the night. Again and again, I teased her with the paddle. Peppering small smacks along her buttocks and down the back of her thighs. Her eyes were closed and her chest moved rapidly as she tried to catch her breath. I threw the paddle down and slid two fingers into her dripping wet pussy.

"You like that, little wolf?"

"Yes, sir."

"Then it seems I'm not doing it right. Pleasure isn't for little whores."

I pushed back from her and pulled my fingers from her cunt. I turned her around, allowing the pulley holding her to twist above her head. Then I pushed down on her back, forcing her ass and hips to shift in my direction as she laid the side of her face on the wall.

"That was for you. Now this is for me," I said, reaching for the thick leather paddle that I loved. I ran it along the inside of her legs and over her drenched pussy. It was shining with her wetness when I pulled it from her body and used it to punish her ass. I could hear her counting as I paddled her backside over and over until her voice was nothing but a whimpering cry. Stepping back, I admired my work. Her back side was an angry color of red and small welts from the layered paddle had formed. I'd enjoy caring for her bruises in the morning, but now I needed to finish what I had planned.

I bent down and undid the shackles that held her legs apart, then I ran my hands up the front of her body, massaging her breasts and peppering them with soft kisses as I reached to undo the restraints holding her arms up. The second they came loose, she fell into my arms and I lifted her gently, placing her in the center of my bed.

"Now, the fun really begins," I whispered into her ear, as I kissed my way along her neck and down her collarbone as she reached up and ran her fingers through my hair.

CHAPTER NINE
MAYA

My mind was a mess. I nearly slipped into the sweet sub space of nothingness when Anton had decided I had enough. I craved the quiet, the peace it brought me and I hoped he knew how badly I wanted that tonight. My body felt weak and needy even though I had already got off in the hallway. I was on edge and the normally soft duvet cover on my backside scratched and burned as Anton covered my body in small little kisses, whispering the praise I so desperately needed to hear.

Something was changing between us tonight. I couldn't put my finger on it, but I could sense it. It was as if our bodies instead of our minds would resolve everything. I loved Anton more than life itself. I always had, I always will. The time I spent away from him nearly destroyed me, but in those moments, the fear of coming back kept me away.

"My beautiful little wolf, you're behaving so good for me. So precious," he said as he reached for the black and gold vibrator next to us. I knew what he planned to do with it and my body screamed in both need and anguish. The torture that I would endure wasn't one I was naïve to. Whenever I pushed him too far, he'd do the same to me. Edging was an evil trick, and he kept it up his sleeve for moments just like this.

"Do you know what I'm going to do to you now?"

I nodded, not trusting my voice.

"Very good," he said as he flipped the vibrator on and ran it over my tight hard nipples. It felt amazing, nearly enough for me to come, and yet if I did, I knew that would be bad.

He turned it off and placed it next to him. Then I watched as he reached for the ropes on the nightstand. Carefully, he pulled the pillows out from under my head and restrained my arms above me, looping the ropes through the metal on the headboard that we had designed ourselves for nights just like tonight. Once he was pleased with my placement, he pushed my legs closed and placed the vibrator so that just the head was touching my clit. He hadn't even turned it on yet, and I fought against the need to come.

The next set of ropes secured my legs and the vibrator in place. I knew what he would say before he even spoke, but his words meant more to me than the actions he took.

"Listen clearly, little wolf. You will not come. Do you understand me?"

I nodded again, "Yes, sir."

"Do you know what will happen if you can't control yourself?"

"You'll stop sir."

"And we don't want that to happen now, do we?"

"No, sir."

"Very good."

He pressed the on button and my body immediately jerked, trying to rid myself of the pleasurable vibrations. Anton knew my body better than I did and he stood next to the bed watching for any sign that I was losing control. I gritted my teeth and stared at him. Trying to remain focused on my job. The only thing I needed to do was not orgasm, yet it felt like an impossible task. I shook my head as a small wave of pleasure tried to creep up and pulled against the ropes that held me. It would leave a mark, but I loved it when that happened and the pain was helping me stay centered.

"I'm so proud of you. Even after all this time, you know exactly what I want. Whose are you, little wolf?"

"Yours, only yours," I grunted out the best I could.

"And what happens when you don't follow the rules?"

"I get punished."

"How?"

"Spankings."

"No, not spankings. You enjoy them too much. Those are for fun. How are you punished?" he asked again when he leaned over me and he sucked my breast into his mouth.

I groaned at the added sensation, but still didn't give in.

"When I don't follow the rules, you don't let me come," I whimpered as he bit down on my nipple, forcing a cry from my lips.

"Very good, my beautiful girl." He rewarded me with his mouth. A deep sensual kiss that nearly pulled my orgasm from me before he began torturing my other breast.

I have no idea how long we were like that. Him playing with me, watching me twitch under his touch while the torture device strapped to my legs caused me to hate the world. Slowly my mind cleared, the surrounding noise became a quiet, dull hum, and I closed my eyes, giving into the moment of pure silence. The trance-like euphoria that came over me was something I missed more than I would admit. The pain was gone, every problem surrounding us didn't exist at that moment, and the only thing in the world was Anton. I felt like I was floating and enveloped in dense white clouds that would never let me fall. My body was slack in my restraints and then I felt a slight give of the ropes around my legs. I couldn't lift my head to look down, but I felt Anton moving my body.

The vibrator never stopped, but he controlled its movements now. I wanted to cry out in joy when he finally penetrated me. His large cock slid into me in one long slow stroke, with the vibrator still between us. He moved at a tormentingly slow pace. I could feel everything as he slid himself between my legs.

When he leaned over me and whispered into my ear, my body followed his demands with no thought from my mind.

"Now, little wolf."

My back arched as my climax hit me like a freight train. I screamed out as tears pooled in my eyes and fell over, spilling down the side of my face onto the sheets below. Anton thrust into me, each stroke harder than the last. My clit went numb as he never let up on the vibrator.

"Fuck!" he grunted, "Mine. You. Are. Mine."

With each thrust of his hips, he growled each word. My climax hadn't slowed down before the next wave came over me. Anton was moving faster and the toy he had between us still hadn't stopped. My body was a useless pile of nothingness when he threw the toy aside and lifted my legs over his shoulders. The angle was deeper and his movements harder until finally he yelled out his release and I crashed over the wave of ecstasy yet again.

I couldn't move and Anton didn't make much effort to either. My legs fell to his hips and his arms reached under me as he held me to his chest. I could feel his cock still twitching inside of me as he held my sweaty body tight to his. I barely breathed, and I didn't dare move a muscle.

Anton laid his head on my chest and the words that he said were something I thought I'd never hear.

"Promise you'll never leave me again."

I couldn't help the tears now. They were uncontrollable as my body shook with emotion and I whispered to him, "Never."

It was impossible to say how long we laid like that. I had lost feeling in my arms long before he released me. Once he pulled out of me and unhooked my restraints, he crawled into bed, holding me and rubbing my arms until the tingling feeling went away.

"We're a mess," he said.

"Yes, we are."

"I need to clean you, but I don't want to leave you here while I run your bath."

"Then don't."

"I was serious about what I said, Maya. You can't leave me again. I don't think I'd survive it. Especially now."

"Because of Dante?"

"No. Because I know what it's like without you and it's not a life worth living."

Anton turned my face to his and placed a kiss on my forehead before moving to stand. Once he was up, he reached for me and cradled me in his arms as he walked to the bathroom. He placed me on the cool marble vanity and went to start the bath. I was certain I must have looked like a nightmare and likely had cum leaking out of me and onto the counter, but I didn't care. I was with Anton, the love of my life, and even though we made each other insane, he was right. A life without him wasn't a life worth living.

"Are you ready?" he asked as he came back for me.

"I think so, but I don't think I can trust my legs just yet."

"Allow me." He scooped me back up into his arms and walked over to the sunken tub. We spent so many nights laying in the water together that I found my heart flutter in joy as he walked down the steps and kneeled down, placing me in the water of the oversized tub. The marks on my backside stung and I must have tensed in his arms because he looked at me with concern.

"I'll take care of your marks. Don't worry, little wolf."

His kisses in the bath were gentle as he washed my body carefully. Anton acted as if he was making up for all the lost aftercare I had been craving since our first night together.

"You know this isn't going to be easy," he said after he had washed my hair and I was laying comfortably in his arms.

"I know."

"Dante says he's not like his father, and I believe him, but that doesn't mean he'll give me the freedom I desire."

"I'm sorry I got you into this position. I'd say I wish I never came, but that would be a lie. If I hadn't shown up, then we wouldn't be here now."

"I'm happy you came to me. I just wish it had been sooner. Working for Dante was always in my future. I had planned on it for years, but when I thought I stood the chance of taking a different path in life, that became the most important thing. It's not anymore. You are the most important thing to me, and if working for the Corsetti family can help me keep you safe, then it's worth it."

I turned in his arms and placed one hand over my name on his chest, then I lifted his hand to place it over his name on mine. "You are my heart, Anton. You always have been."

He closed the space between us and kissed me.

"We need to get out so I can get you dressed and taken care of," he murmured.

"Can I sleep with you tonight?"

"Yes, but my bed is a mess. We'll stay the night in your room and tomorrow I'll have the bed moved out of there. We only need one bed and it will be mine. I'll have the decorators set your bedroom up as a living area. That way, you still have your space, but mine will always be yours as well."

Anton lifted me from the bath even though I told him I was certain I could climb out myself. He placed me on a towel he had laid out and then began drying my body. When he finished, we moved to the mirror, and I watched as he brushed out my long hair and rubbed ointment into my wrists and backside where I had welts and rope burn.

"I didn't mean to be so rough with you tonight. How are you feeling?"

Absently, I reached for my side and pressed on my ribs. I winced at the pain that I had easily ignored while we played. "Fine, as long as I don't poke them."

He reached into the medicine cabinet and pulled a bottle of pills out. "Here, take two of these. They are just over the counter, not the pain meds you were taking before. I don't want you to wake up more sore than you need to."

I did as he asked and then followed him into my room. He pulled down the covers and slid in behind me. When he turned the last light out, he pulled my back to his front and held me close.

"Anton?"

"Yes, little wolf."

"I love you."

"I love you too. Now get some sleep. It will be morning soon."

CHAPTER TEN
ANTON

"We have a problem."

It had been two weeks of utter shit and we finally tracked down a lead at another hotel in hopes it would bring us close enough to find Tommy. We had fucked up enough of his guys to fill a mausoleum, but we still hadn't gotten to him and Maya was growing restless stuck at home.

"What now?"

"Where's your phone?"

"At the house, I only brought a burner. Why?"

"They have Maya."

The blood was pounding in my ears so loud I couldn't even hear what Nico was saying as he picked up the phone that started buzzing in his hand. He took off running toward the exit of the hotel and I followed close behind. Before I realized what was going on, Nico was behind the driver's seat of my SUV and had his hand out for the keys. I held them out to him and he started the car and pulled out, nearly hitting the valet who yelled at me for leaving it there when I came in.

"How did this happen?" I growled out through gritted teeth when I could finally talk.

"Marybeth is in the hospital. Nothing serious, but they want to keep her for observation. He knocked her out to get to Maya. Dante and Ares found her when they got to the house."

"How did they—?"

Fuck. We had been messy, cocky really, as we took down each of their guys. I never hid the fact that Maya was with me, but I never would have thought he'd go after her at my house. Nico kept talking, and I just nodded my head. It was impossible to process everything he was saying. I had no idea where we were going, and I didn't care. As long as it brought me closer to getting Maya back, nothing mattered.

"There is an auction tonight."

I snapped my head in his direction. "Where?"

"Ares texted me the address. Dante planned to be there, but now they are certain Tommy's planning to sell Maya tonight. The Romano's just released the catalog and there is a woman listed that fits her description."

"Why would they do that? Wouldn't it be smarter to just move her? Send her to another auction outside of the city?"

"Maybe. But Tommy's never been smart. Besides, he's not running things, the Romano's are. That's why we were supposed to go tonight. I told you they've been after us to get into the business, but Dante refused. They wouldn't let up, so we were going to see what it was all about. The more info we had on the situation, the better."

"So we go. We fucking kill all of them and we take Maya back."

"I'm always ready for a bloodbath, but every crime family on the east coast will be represented. Dante will put a bullet through your head if you do something that stupid."

"How do we get her back?"

"We get to her before she's there."

Nico swerved onto a side street and two other blacked out SUVs came up behind us. The window tint was so dark I couldn't tell who they were, but Nico smiled then put his foot down on the gas.

"Now we get to have some fun," he said with the evil laugh that, after all this time, still creeped me out. I had known Dante, Nico and Ares since we were kids. Crime connected our families, each of us innocent in our own rights until we weren't. Things with Nico changed the summer after high school. All three of them went to Italy and when they returned, something had shifted in him. Something deviant came to the surface and never disappeared. Spilling blood became his only purpose. Mindless, numbing killing turned into torture, and now he controlled the city with his two best friends. If you ran into anyone of them in a dark alley you'd panic, but Nico is the man you shy away from on a sunny afternoon in Central Park.

Once we hit the highway, the SUV behind us moved in front and Nico followed close behind.

"Ares?"

"Yeah, Dante is behind us."

"Is there a plan?"

"Drive fast. Track down Tommy. Get your girl."

Death would be too quick for Tommy Marconi. I sat in the passenger's seat contemplating handing the asshole over to Nico to let him do with him whatever he wished. Maybe then he'd piss himself in fear and beg for his life. I had so many questions, but my anger over rode all of them. Right now I was trusting The Dark Kings with my entire world.

Ares' SUV slowed as he took an exit ramp. We followed until it came to a stop on the side of the road. Nico pulled up alongside him and pulled the window down.

"He stopped a quarter mile up."

"How many are with him?"

"No idea. Two cars, not sure how many are in each. He already delivered his women to the Romano's auction, but the timing isn't right. He picked up Maya after the delivery."

"How do you know she's with him?" I asked.

"She's on tonight's auction block, so he would need to get her there in time. Here, look," Ares said, throwing a pile of papers at me through the window. I looked down at the mess and I couldn't believe what I saw. They were print-outs and order forms for a silent auction. They had posted pictures and details of each girl on a dark website. Ares printed it all and as I flipped through the pages, one face stood out. Maya. It was a picture from before Eddie split her eyebrow and bruised her face. She was smiling, but her eyes were empty, void of all emotion. Where and when he took it was a mystery to me, but clearly he had been planning this for longer than he let on.

"Let's go."

Ares pulled ahead, but this time, Dante passed us as well. Tommy would see us coming a mile away, but we didn't have time to be covert. The auction started in an hour, according to the forms in my lap. There was no way Maya was going to that place.

"We could always just buy her back."

"No. I don't want her there. She doesn't need memories of being sold off like a prized whore among a bunch of innocent girls. It would break her."

"She doesn't strike me as someone who breaks easily."

I looked away as the thoughts of Maya's only true breakdown flooded my mind. The day she lost our child was the worst day we had ever experienced together. The pains started in the middle of the night. She was already five months along. We thought we were in the clear, but we weren't. Holding her while she delivered our child, who would never take a breath, was the hardest thing I've ever done in my life. Nico was right. There wasn't much that got to her, but that broke her. It broke us.

Ares pulled into a gas station behind a white panel van, and Nico and Dante blocked either side. I grabbed the door and went to jump out, but Nico pulled me back.

"Hold on."

"Fuck you."

"Look," he said, pointing inside the convenience store. There was Tommy with two of his men, laughing and joking as if they didn't have a care in the world.

Ares knocked on the window, and I rolled it down. "She's in the van."

"You're sure?" I asked, looking at the one person no one could escape even if they tried. Ares Sabino was a manipulative, cocky asshole, but he had every right to be.

I was good with documents, but this man was a master at tracking and hacking. He didn't respond, but pointed to the guy who had just got out of his SUV. He was sliding a slim piece of metal between the window and the door frame. I opened the door, ready to get to Maya as soon as I could. I stood next to him and watched as Dante, Ares and Nico all walked around the cars and stood next to each other, facing the clear glass door of the shop.

"Well, well, well, what do we have here?" My skin crawled as I heard Tommy's voice. I turned to see him approach Dante with his two men as they unholstered their weapons. "How did I get so lucky that I get a personal visit from all three of The Dark Kings?"

"We have a few questions for you."

"For me? Dante Corsetti left his ivory tower just to talk to little old me?" Tommy's mocking voice was pissing everyone off. The tension notched up to an uncomfortable level when I finally heard the door open. Luckily, with the way everyone parked, Tommy's men couldn't see what was happening. Two other guys stepped out of Dante's car and then everything moved at the same time. I pushed my way into the back of the van to find Maya bound and unconscious. She was breathing fine as I took a knife from my boot and cut her free. When I lifted her into my arms and pulled her out of the van, I could hear the telltale sounds of gunshots being let off, muffled only by the silencers attached to Ares' and Nico's weapons. Tommy's two men were on the ground, and Dante had a gun pressed into his forehead.

There was no one around except the kid working inside and he must have been hiding under the counter because he was nowhere to be seen.

"I told you, Tommy, all I wanted to do was talk," Dante ground out when the gunfire stopped, "But now you've gone and made a mess. You're going to pay for that."

"Fuck off, Dante. You think you're so powerful, but you aren't shit."

"Yet I'm the one standing here with a gun to your head while your latest paycheck is being removed from your transport vehicle. Really, why do you even bother trying? It's got to be tiring losing to me all the fucking time."

When Tommy didn't answer, Dante nodded his head in Nico's direction. I watched from the back seat of my Escalade as he grabbed Tommy and pulled his wrists behind his back. With Ares' help, he shoved him into the back of the other SUV Dante had been driving. I couldn't see well from where I was, but the next thing I heard was two car doors close and Nico speeding off back toward the highway.

Maya was laying in my arms and I wanted to shake her awake, yell at her to come back to me but it was useless. I had no idea if they had knocked her out physically or used a sedative. Both were dangerous, so I did my best to hold her still.

"It's okay, little wolf. It will all be over soon," I whispered into her ear as Ares got into the driver's seat. He started it and turned back to me. "The guys will clean this up. Nico is taking Tommy back to our house for you. Where do you want me to take Maya?"

"Home. Take us both home."

The ride to the house was quiet, other than a few calls Ares made. One to their clean-up team, another to Dante, who had taken off in the opposite direction. He still planned to get to the auction before everything started. I had him call Dr. Anders to have him meet us at the house. Considering he was not only my personal doctor, but also the Corsetti's, that worked to my advantage on nights like this. When we got to the house, there was a company there fixing my front door. It looked like it had exploded on its hinges.

"I called them to come out before we left and authorized the work. I figured it was better than plywood."

"Thanks," I said as I pulled Maya's body to mine and walked up the steps to the house. Ares followed me all the way to our bedroom and stood in the doorway while I placed her gently on the bed.

"It must have been a sedative. Otherwise, she'd be up by now."

"Maybe, I hope so at least."

"She's breathing okay, besides it's Maya. She would have fought like hell to keep them from taking her from you and she doesn't have a scratch on her."

I nodded and walked into the bathroom to get a wet washcloth to wipe her face. When I got back, Ares was gone.

"Maya, come on, baby. Wake up, for me," I urged, as I held the cool washcloth to her skin, "I need you, please, little wolf."

It was useless. She looked as if she had been asleep for hours. Dr. Anders' voice traveled down the hallway when he arrived.

"We're in here," I called out to him.

I was sitting on the side of the bed holding Maya's hand when he came in.

"I don't know what they gave her," I said as he approached.

"Okay, let me take a look."

I stepped back and watched as he examined Maya. "How long ago did you find her like this?"

"About forty-five minutes, maybe more. I don't know how long she was unconscious before that."

"I'd like to get her to a hospital to run some blood tests, but I assume that's not an option?"

"No."

"Help me move her. I think I see something."

I lifted Maya into my arms so he could look at a spot on her neck that I hadn't noticed.

"There's a needle mark here." I watched as he pushed her tank top up and looked at her back. "And another here. The first dose must have worn off, and they gave it to her again. That's a good sign."

"How long will it take?"

"I really don't know, since I have no idea what it was. There are drugs I could give her to counteract the effects, but without knowing the original drug and dosage, I don't want to risk it. I can set up an IV with fluids and that will help keep her hydrated and hopefully move things through her system faster."

"Thank you."

"You'll need to lay her down again," he added, placing a hand on my shoulder, "She'll be okay. Just give her some time."

I wasn't much of a wait-and-see guy, and watching Maya laying there was killing me. The only other time in our lives that I couldn't solve a problem for her was when we lost our baby. Everything else I could do, I fixed things for her. That was my role in our relationship, but now I was stuck.

"Why don't you go get yourself a drink? I'll be with her for a bit, setting everything up, and won't leave until you get back."

I nodded and headed out into the main part of the house. The guys who had replaced my front doors were packing up to go, and I found Ares with four guys in my kitchen.

"Hey, how's she doing?"

"Still out of it," I said as I went to the refrigerator and grabbed a beer, "Doc says she'll be okay. We just have to wait."

"I'm sorry, man, this should have never happened."

I didn't bother agreeing or disagreeing with Ares. There was no point.

"Dante asked me to leave these guys here. They can stay outside if you want or I can split them between the house and the property. You would just need to give one of them access to the security room."

"Yeah, that's fine. If they don't mind watching monitors all night."

"Nico has Tommy at the house for you. He'll keep hi m... entertained until you are ready."

"I'm not leaving Maya until she wakes up and feels better."

"I get it. I also called Marybeth's sister. She is driving in from Jersey to stay with her until she's released in the morning."

"This is all so fucked up."

"I know. It could have been worse, though. If I wasn't monitoring your alarm system, then we wouldn't have known about the break-in. I know you're not happy working for us, but there are some advantages."

"Yeah, I know. I need to get back to Maya. Tell Nico I'll be in touch when things are back to normal around here."

"Keep us posted." Ares stood and reached a hand forward to shake mine. Then he turned and made his way through my house and out the front doors as if he had been there a million times before. I walked the guy down to my security room and unlocked it, gave him a quick rundown of how it all worked, and by the time I got back upstairs, the others were gone. I assumed they'd taken their places outside for the night and went back to Maya.

The doc had finished and was packing up. I thanked him and when he left, I crawled into bed next to Maya. Pulling her body to me without jostling the arm with her IV.

"Come back to me, Maya. Please."

CHAPTER ELEVEN

MAYA

My body was heavy, and I was so hot my skin felt like it was on fire. I shifted my head and then quickly raised my hand to it when the pain of a million needles rushed to my forehead, causing the worst headache I had ever had. When I moved my arm, I had an entirely different pain assail me. I cracked my eyes open and looked at my arm in the darkness. It was late, very late from the looks of things. I was home, Anton was with me, but I had an IV in my arm. That's when it all came rushing back.

Tommy, his men, Marybeth, the fear of never seeing Anton again all bombarded me at once and I choked out a cry of relief that it was over. The tears that fell came so fast I didn't even bother to wipe them away and by the time I gasped for air, Anton's face came into my line of vision.

"You're okay. Just breathe Maya, I've got you," he said as he pulled me tighter into his chest and ran his fingers through my hair.

I grasped onto him as if he were the lifeline I so desperately needed. His warm body and the spicy, smooth scent of him surrounded me as I fell apart in his arms.

"I thought I lost you," he whispered, and I only cried harder. He sat up and pulled me onto his lap, rocking me back and forth in a soothing motion until my breathing finally evened out.

"I'm so sorry," I said once I finally got my voice back, "I'm so, so, sorry."

"You have nothing to be sorry about. Everything is okay now. It's over."

"Is he dead?"

"Not yet, but soon."

My body tensed at the thought that he could come after me again. "How did he get away?"

"He didn't. Nico has him. The only reason he's still alive is because I wanted Ares to bring us home until you woke up. Nico is holding him at the Villa for me."

"I want to come."

"No."

"I'm not staying here alone."

"I'm not going tonight. I want to make sure you are okay, and Marybeth will get released in the morning. Once our house is back in order and everyone is taken care of, I'll deal with Tommy."

"Is she okay? I can't believe I didn't ask you right away."

"She's just fine. Her sister is with her and I texted them both a couple of hours ago. Other than a headache and a ton of worry over you, she is just fine."

"Can we call her?"

"Why don't we get you some food and water in you first, okay?"

"When did you change my clothes?" I asked, noticing I was dressed in my favorite cozy pajamas.

"Right after Dr. Anders left. The IV was tricky to work around, but I managed."

"Thank you. I don't think I'm hungry, though. What time is it?"

Anton reached for his phone on the nightstand. "Four a.m."

"How long have I been out?"

"Too long. They must have fucked up when they dosed you the second time. There is no way you would have been awake in time for the auction."

I shivered at the mention of what could have happened to me. "I have about a million questions."

"I'll answer them, but only once you try to eat a little something. I'll get some dry toast and crackers for you. The Doc said you'd might be nauseous when you woke up."

"He wasn't wrong about that."

"I'll be right back. Let me get you some things to settle your stomach."

When Anton left for the kitchen, I tested my strength and shuffled my way into the bathroom. My body felt so heavy it was hard to move, but my bladder wasn't going to wait much longer. I walked slowly and held onto furniture my whole way there, but I was pleased with myself that I had made it to the bathroom on my own. After taking care of business, I sat on the stool Anton bought for me in front of the built-in vanity. My face was pale and my eyes were all glassy. I wasn't sure what they had given me, but it certainly wasn't out of my system yet. I reached for a brush and tried to lift my arms to pull my hair down from the messy bun it was in, but the movement was too much.

"Maya, where are you?" Anton's panicked voice made me jump.

"In here."

He was at the door of the bathroom in an instant with a look of terror on his face. "I thought... fuck," he said, turning from me and slamming his fist into the wall just outside of the bathroom. The sound made me jump a second time as his anger had broke and he roared with rage. I wanted to go to him, but I wasn't certain I'd make it. The little I had done took too much out of me, so all I could do was sit and wait for him to come back.

"Anton?" I asked once he had quieted.

It took him a minute, but he stepped into the bathroom, barely composed. "I'm sorry. I didn't know where you were."

I reached a hand out for him and held my breath as he came to me. He got to his knees and wrapped his arms around my center, laying his head in my lap. Never in our lives had I seen him so vulnerable, so hurt over what we had endured.

"I'm sorry. I didn't mean to scare you. I had to use the bathroom, but it took too much energy, so I sat down here. When you called for me, I was going to brush out my hair while I waited for you."

"I can't lose you again," he said as his arms tightened around me.

"You won't."

Eventually, his grip loosened, and he stood, reaching for my hairbrush. He pulled my hair out of the tie that was holding it back and let it fall down my back as he brushed it slowly. I closed my eyes and relished in the attention from the man I loved more than anything else in the world. When he was done, he called Dr. Anders and got the okay to remove my IV. I wish I could say this was the first time we dealt with something like this, but it wasn't, and it likely wouldn't be, the last. The lives we lived were difficult. Even with him working for Dante, there would always be a risk that he could get hurt. Hospitals weren't really a thing for people like us. I mean, if there was no choice, then of course we went, but it took a lot of bribes to keep reporting to a minimum. Removing an IV was nothing compared to removing a bullet from someone, and he had done that more than once when we were young.

Once we were done in the bathroom, he picked me up and brought me back to bed. For the first time ever, I was grateful I didn't have to make my way there on my own. I sunk down into the pillows as he covered me up with the blankets and I knew in that moment I wasn't going to stay awake long.

"The tea I made you went cold, but here, drink some water."

He gave me a bottle of water and a plate of toast. I couldn't get much more than a few bites in before my eyes were closing. I felt Anton take the plate from my hands and heard him place it on the nightstand. After that, I gave in to the sleep that was forcing itself on me.

I slept through the next morning, which wasn't much of a surprise. When I finally woke up, it was after one o'clock and Anton was still laying in bed next to me.

"Good morning, sunshine."

"Ughhhh...." I grumbled as I moved my body, testing out the soreness of everything, "How long did I sleep?"

"As long as you needed to," he said, leaning over and placing a kiss on my forehead, "How are you feeling?"

"Better, I think."

"What hurts?"

I smiled. "Nothing I can't deal with."

Anton put his laptop down on the nightstand and reached for me. I willingly rolled into his arms and let him hold me.

"This was a close one, wasn't it?"

"It was."

"Too close."

"I would have found you. I'd burn the entire city down until I did, little wolf."

"I love you."

"I love you, too," he said, pressing his lips to mine, which only reminded me I hadn't brushed my teeth in over twenty-four hours.

"I'll be back. I need to use the bathroom and get cleaned up."

"Let me take you," he said, pulling away and standing up.

"No, I can do it. I feel a lot better this morning."

"Maya, I'm not leaving you, so either I carry you or we walk together."

Anton reached an arm out to me, and I took it. I was still shaky on my feet, but not nearly as weak as the night before.

"When you're done, Marybeth would love to see you."

"She's back?"

"Yes, she got discharged this morning and she and her sister are out in the living room. I told her sister to stay a few days if she'd like, since she seems to be the only person who can get Marybeth to stop working. As soon as she walked in, she started wiping down counters and asking what everyone wanted for breakfast."

I laughed because that was exactly how Marybeth was, and I loved her for it.

"We'll go down and eat. I can make her lunch for a change."

"Yeah, I don't think so. Let's get you in the shower and then I'll order us all something. Everyone could do with a day of rest around here."

"Didn't you sleep?"

"Not much."

I reached my hand up and ran it over the stubble on his chin. I was so worried about myself that I hadn't really looked at Anton. The unstoppable man that I loved looked as if he had been through hell and back.

"I really am sorry."

Anton reached for my hand and placed a kiss on the inside of my wrist. "Stop apologizing to me. I won't hear it anymore. We have both fucked up enough over the years. My only goal now is to keep you safe and loved for the rest of your life."

"Forever?"

"Forever."

"But what if—?"

"Nope, no more what if's. We have everything we need right here. Once I get this shit with Tommy behind us, I'm taking you to the courthouse and marrying you. Then I'm going to do everything I can to give you that rainbow baby

I promised you. We deserve happiness, Maya. In a world of so much shit, it's our turn for some hope."

I could feel the tears pooling in my eyes as I looked up at him. I said a little internal prayer that we would finally catch a break. He was right. Our world was shit. Ever since he befriended the little bruised girl in elementary school, we had faced one challenge after another. We decided things we thought would free us from our past, but they never did. When Anton turned twenty-one, he killed my father. He beat the man to death for what he had done to me, but the result of it all ended up with us being in debt to his mother's family. Two twenty-one-year-old kids hadn't thought much about disposing of a body. That was the first time we made a decision together that put us in debt to someone else. Now he owed his life to Dante for helping me get away from the mess I made for us.

"What about Dante?"

"What about him?"

"Will you keep working for him?"

He let out a deep breath. "I don't think he lied to me when he said he wasn't his father. He is making moves and decisions I understand and I can support. The truth is Maya, I think we both know working for Dante Corsetti was always in my future. Even though I pretended it wasn't. We'll be okay. He knows my intentions for our future and won't call on me more than what's needed. Especially once we start our family."

"You are my everything."

Anton smiled down at me and went to lower his head, but I turned my face and he got stuck with my cheek. "I still haven't brushed my teeth."

He laughed and placed tiny kisses all over my face until I couldn't stop smiling. When he stepped away to start the shower, I watched as he stripped away his clothes. Each tattoo on his body had meant something important to him. Many of mine were simply things I thought were pretty, but his had meaning. I watched as his muscles rippled with his movement and my gaze caught scars that held memories of our past. Most were terrible, some were funny. The one he'd never forgive me for was when I stabbed him because I thought he was cheating on me. I let out a slight laugh, and it caught his attention.

"Are you laughing at me?"

"No. Not you... me. I'm just remembering how you got that scar," I said, pointing at the jagged mark on his side.

"That's still not funny."

"Oh, come on! It was years ago."

"Maya, you stabbed me."

"So. I'd do it again too. That cock of yours belongs to me... forever. You just told me so."

He reached for me and began stripping my clothes away. "It's always been yours, little wolf. Even when you stabbed me in a state of insanity."

CHAPTER TWELVE

ANTON

"I'm still not comfortable with you being here," I said to Maya as we pulled through the guard gate of the Corsetti compound. Their primary home was outside of the city in a wooded area tucked away from prying eyes. Although the guys had properties all over the world, including a few apartments in the city, this seemed to be where they spent most of their time. It surprised me they brought Tommy here rather than somewhere less risky. However, the truth of the matter was, Tommy wasn't going to walk out of here again, so it didn't really matter.

"I understand, but I told you I feel fine and I'm not letting you do this alone."

I reached for her hand, thankful she was still with me after the shitstorm the last few weeks had been. Late last night we sat up and she told me everything that had happened throughout the three years we were apart. It killed me to hear how much she had suffered without me and knowing I was just as bad off without her. I made a promise to her that the future would be different. We both deserved more than what we gave each other. Which is why when she told me she wanted to look into Tommy's eyes as the life drained from his body, I agreed to let her come. It appeared my little wolf had a taste for blood and a few words she wanted to share with the man who nearly ruined her life.

I pulled around the large circular driveway and parked in front of the double doors. A man dressed in black with an ear piece answered it and pointed in the direction of the living room. I had been here numerous times over the years and yet every time I came, the place overwhelmed me. Dante's apartment in the city was modern, light and nearly empty, but his home here had been the Corsetti family home for many years, and in every corner were memories of their time there together.

Maya sat on the couch while I stood by her. I had done a decent job of keeping my anger under control until this point, but the closer I got to seeing Tommy again, the harder it was to reel it all in.

"Thank god you're here," Ares said as he approached us from a hallway on the right, "I'm getting sick of Nico's complaining ass. He's had fun playing with his new toy, but he's grown impatient and won't shut up about it."

I shook his hand and watched as he leaned down to kiss Maya on the cheek. It shouldn't bother me, but knowing Ares was the playboy of the group always made me anxious when he was close to her.

"Come on, I'll bring you to them."

I reached for Maya and helped her to stand as we made our way through to the back of the house. He opened a large sliding glass door that led out to the courtyard in the back. The property was overly wooded, but the backyard was a perfectly manicured oasis with a pond and gazebo on one side and a large pool with an attached cabaña on the other. Once we made our way past it, we approached a smaller building just past the tree line of the property, and Ares reached for the door.

"Dante made Nico build this. The noise and ... um, smells that came from the basement were getting to be a bit much. He wanted it all moved outside before Valentina gets here."

"Valentina Romano?" Maya asked.

A soft smile came over Ares' face. "Yes. It shouldn't be long now."

Maya looked up at me, and I shook my head slightly. She knew some of what was going on with the Romano's but I hadn't shared with her the depth of the situation. Now certainly wasn't the time.

"Tommy boy! You have visitors!" Ares called out as Nico stepped into view. One look at the place and I knew immediately why Dante wanted this moved outside. The stench was the first thing that hit me. It smelled of blood and urine and, with a cursory glance toward Tommy, I could see why. Nico had him chained up against a concrete wall. His clothes were in tatters and his face was a bloody mess. He smelled as if he should already be dead or at least begging to die. He didn't beg, though. Instead, he threw out curses and slurs the second he opened his eyes.

"You fucking little whore! This is all your fault. When I get out of here, I'm coming for you. I'll fuck you until you beg for mercy and then strangle the life out of you."

I lunged forward, only to be stopped by Nico's grip on my arm. "Slow down, man. Let's make sure we have time to enjoy this."

His voice was low, and his eyes were glazed over with blood lust. Nico lived for shit like this.

"Maya, good to see you. It's been a while."

"Good to see you too, Nico." she said, but her eyes never left Tommy. He was glaring at her and running his tongue over his teeth like some kind of sick monster looking to intimidate her. I reached for her arm, but she stepped out of my hold and walked to a table that was set up on the side of the room. I hadn't noticed it before, but it must have caught her eye. She walked along the side of it, slowly dragging her finger over every knife, rope, and torture device Nico had there.

"You're going to kill me?" she said in a soft sing-songy voice I hadn't heard before, "That's what you think, after all this time? You know, at one point, I was thankful you let me work for you. I was convinced, just like all the other girls, that you were the lesser of two evils. But that wasn't the case, was it Tommy?"

She picked up a dagger with a decorative handle. One I'd seen Nico carry often, and she held it up in front of her face, testing the sharpness of it with the tip of her finger. When she pulled it back, she had a small drop of blood on it and stuck it in her mouth, slowly sucking it away.

"You see, Tommy, there are a lot of evil things in this world, but men... men are the most evil of them all. Even the good ones go bad given the right opportunity, but you never even had an opportunity to be good. I pity you for that. Now you will die today wondering what it would have been like to get what you always wanted. You got none of it, Tommy. Money and power were the only things that drove you and now here you are, standing in your own piss and blood, chained to a wall and about to die."

Maya had continued to stroll in his direction as she spoke. Now she was less than a foot away from him and he arched his body forward, screaming at her, but she didn't move a muscle. I wanted to go to her, tell her I'd take care of it. That she didn't need to do this, but I couldn't. She needed this more than I did. The dagger moved quickly. If I hadn't been watching, I would have missed it. She struck him in the side, twisted it and yanked it back out. Tommy screamed as blood pooled on the floor and his body went slack.

"Look at me Tommy. I want you to look into my eyes and remember me in death. Remember what you did to me, to all of us who trusted you with our safety. Instead of safety, we got raped, beaten and then sold off to the highest bidder. You are a disgusting piece of shit."

Maya ran the knife along the side of his face and down his neck, cutting into his skin as she went.

"Children, Tommy. Some of those girls were babies, and you destroyed them," she said as she stabbed him in his other side.

He was losing consciousness quickly, but she wasn't nearly done. I looked at Nico and he nodded before walking over to the table and picked up a glass of water. He approached Maya and placed a hand on her arm, breaking the trance she was in.

"Let me," he breathed as he threw a glass of water in Tommy's face and then held smelling salts under his nose. Tommy grunted, but opened his eyes.

"She's not done with you yet," Nico said as he stepped back and nodded to Maya.

Watching her go through this was torture. The effects of killing someone weren't something that ever left you. With time it got easier, but just the other night she woke up dreaming of the night she killed the man who had attacked her. There was no doubt this would fuck her up once it was over, but I had to let it happen and be there for her when reality set in.

"Do you remember Anna? The sweet redhead who got knocked up by one of your Johns? What happened to her, Tommy? What did you do with her?"

He shook his head and then lowered it to his chest as if he couldn't even hold it up any longer. Maya reached forward and grabbed his filthy hair, holding his head up and she asked again.

"Where is she Tommy?"

"Dead."

Maya dropped his head and stepped back. The dagger slipped from her hand and crashed to the concrete floor with a loud clatter. She turned to me with anger in her eyes and I knew what she needed before she even said the words.

"Kill him."

I reached for my gun, released the safety, held it up and without even flinching placed a bullet into the head of the man who nearly ruined my girl.

Nico started clapping as I handed my gun to Ares. I got to Maya just in time. Her knees gave out, and the tears began as her body shook. I scooped her up into my arms and walked towards the door we entered. Ares wasn't far behind and opened it.

"We'll take care of this, you take care of her," he said, placing a hand on my shoulder as I stepped outside into the shining afternoon light.

I walked toward the gazebo as Maya clung to me. Once I took a seat, I held her tightly, thankful everything was over. Her sobs slowed, and I pushed her hair back from her face. Needing to see her clearly, I kissed her. I poured every bit of myself into that kiss, proving to her how our love got us through. The same love that pushed us through so much shit when we were younger would get us through this as well.

I had no idea how long we stayed like that. It was long enough for Ares to come out and find us.

"You guys okay?"

"We will be," I said.

"Do you want to use the guest quarters to get cleaned up?"

I looked down at Maya. She was splattered with blood, but nothing major. "What do you think, little wolf? Do you want to head home or change first?"

She looked up at me with a small smile. "Let's go home."

We didn't talk on the way home or while we showered and changed. There was a comfortable silence between the two of us, and I let it stay that way for as long as I could. It was only late afternoon, but once we got cleaned up Maya crawled into bed and I joined her. Now that Tommy was dead, we could take a deep breath. There was one thing that bothered me, something I needed an answer to before we finally put this all to rest.

"You never mentioned Anna before."

Maya stiffened in my arms, "She was the girl who I met at the diner. The one who helped me get started and adjusted to the job. She said she was eighteen, but I always suspected she was younger. An old soul for such a young girl. When she found out she was pregnant, she was terrified. I encouraged her to keep the baby, to tell Tommy she was done. I wanted to help her. We talked about getting an apartment together. I told her I could help her raise the baby while she went back to school. But then the night she went to meet with Tommy, she disappeared. There were rumors she ran away, but I didn't believe it. She was a friend, Anton, and now she's dead."

"I had no idea."

"I didn't want you to know. But looking at him this afternoon, I knew if I didn't ask I'd always wonder."

"I'm going to take you away from all this. We leave in the morning."

She turned to me, "How?"

"Easy. We get on a plane and we fly away. I already talked to Dante. We'll go to Italy. We haven't been since we were kids and I'd like to learn more about my father's country."

"But the club, you have work. What about Marybeth?"

"Everything is taken care of. We can stay for as long as we need to."

"I think I'd like that."

"Then it's settled. Tomorrow morning, we will go to the courthouse. Once we are married, we will leave."

"You are serious?"

"Always."

Maya pulled me to her and the sweet feel of her lips on mine reminded me of how lucky I was. Some people spend their entire lives looking for their soul mate, and I found mine when we were only kids. I'd never lied to her. I'd burn down the world if I needed to save her and I knew without a doubt she'd do the same for me.

BEFORE YOU GO...

Do you want to know more about The Dark Kings? What would you do if three men showed up in the middle of the night promising to take care of you after burning your house to the ground? Learn what Valentina decides buy reading Lust: A Dark Arranged Marriage Mafia Romance today.
READ LUST TODAY!
Get it here: Lust

About the Author

USA Today Best Selling Romance Author Nikki Rome has been a romance junky since a young age. As a girl she reached for book after book, looking for that happily ever after she always believed in. She loves all forms of romance and you can find her latest read not far from her reach. Nikki writes contemporary romance with a touch of danger and kink. Her love of realistic characters who face real problems provides a story that touches the hearts of many. As a writer, reader and lover of words, it only made sense that she publish her stories.

Now years later she owns and manages Smut Lovers: The Community. A group of like minded individuals that come together to talk about their love of all things smut. You can find her hosting Smut Lovers: The Podcast or running Smut Lovers: The Conference. Either way you know she'll always be talking about her love of books.

www.NikkiRome.com
Facebook

www.ingramcontent.com/pod-product-compliance
Lightning Source LLC
Chambersburg PA
CBHW031057310726
48969CB00007B/2314